A p   of
resp   be
esta   cs
of getting along. This is the book that shows you ...

   *Familiarize your pet with children
   *Know when supervision is necessary
   *Recognize and handle problems that develop
   *Help your child appreciate the joys and
    responsibilities of having a pet
   *Select the right pet for your family
    and much more

        BECOMING BEST FRIENDS
   Building a Loving Relationship Between
        Your Pet and Your Child

Also From Berkley Books

DOG TRAINING MY WAY
Barbara Woodhouse

FIRST AID AND HEALTH CARE FOR CATS
Dr. Charles Bell

FIRST AID AND HEALTH CARE FOR DOGS
Dr. Charles Bell

HAPPY KITTENS, HAPPY CATS
Mordecai Siegal

YOUR NEW BEST FRIEND:
EVERYTHING THE NEW DOG OWNER NEEDS TO KNOW
Mordecai Siegal

Becoming Best Friends

Building a Loving Relationship Between Your Pet and Your Child

JANE E. LEON, D.V.M.
& LISA D. HOROWITZ

BERKLEY BOOKS, NEW YORK

BECOMING BEST FRIENDS

A Berkley Book / published by arrangement with
Pecos Press

PRINTING HISTORY
Pecos Press edition published 1991
Berkley edition / October 1993

All rights reserved.
Copyright © 1991 by Jane E. Leon, D.V.M., and Lisa Horowitz.
This book may not be reproduced in whole or in part,
by mimeograph or any other means, without permission.
For information address: The Berkley Publishing Group,
200 Madison Avenue, New York, New York 10016.

ISBN: 0-425-13956-5

BERKLEY®
Berkley Books are published by The Berkley Publishing Group,
200 Madison Avenue, New York, New York 10016.
BERKLEY and the "B" design
are trademarks belonging to Berkley Publishing Corporation.

PRINTED IN THE UNITED STATES OF AMERICA

10 9 8 7 6 5 4 3 2 1

To Art, Melanie, Sherman and
the memory of Chrissy,
my best friend
—Jane E. Leon, D.V.M.

To my beloved husband, Lewis,
and our two daughters,
Esther and Rivka
—Lisa D. Horowitz

Preface

It was just over twelve months ago when my dog took a nip at my child. Beckett, my lovable Labrador Retriever, tried to bite my eighteen month old daughter, Esther. I immediately separated Beckett from Esther by putting the dog in the backyard. My husband wanted to make the separation permanent; he wanted the dog out of the house for good.

I was not convinced that such a drastic measure was necessary. I felt that, with proper help, I could remedy the situation. My veterinarian, Jane E. Leon, D.V.M., writes and records the nationally syndicated radio feature, "Pets and People," for the Associated Press. I remembered that Dr. Leon had covered how to handle problems between pets and children in one of her shows. I gave her a call.

Jane was very willing to help. We discussed my problem for a while over the phone. She then came to my house and observed the interactions among Beckett, Esther and me. Jane concluded that Beckett was anxious about her changing status in the family. As Esther grew increasingly active, she required more of my attention; I had less time to spend with the dog. In addition, my child began to give unsolicited attention to the animal. Beckett felt threatened and struck back.

In further discussions with Jane, I learned that

most dogs give signals when a problem is developing. She told me the most common signs. As I thought back on the previous months, I remembered that Beckett had displayed a few of them. My dog had been showing me that there was a problem but I did not recognize the warning.

Jane suggested some steps and exercises to solve the dilemma. Now, Beckett and Esther are constant companions. Jane did more than just help the two of them become best friends. She kept our pet from being unceremoniously drummed out of the family. Her help also enabled Beckett to adapt easily when our second daughter, Rivka, was added to the family.

If a dog as sweet as Beckett could try to hurt a child, I knew that other families must be having the same problem. That was when Jane and I decided to write this book. We combined her knowledge of animals with my experience with children. I am very pleased with the result.

I would like to thank Jane for letting me work with her on this project. But I am even more grateful for her contribution towards the wonderful relationship that now exists between my dog and my child.

Lisa D. Horowitz
Bethesda, Maryland
August 1991

Contents

Becoming Best Friends

Part I

BEFORE
Your Child Arrives

Chapter One
Animals and People

You should plan on keeping your pet after the arrival of your new baby. The relationship between a domestic animal and its human family has many benefits for both. For the animal, the people in the household offer a stable, secure and happy home. To the people, the animal gives unconditional love and companionship that can have a positive effect on your family's physical and emotional health. This love is reassuring to both children and adults.

Benefits For a Child

Pets and children belong together. For children, pets are more than just animals; they are often close companions and friends. A dog or cat can offer feelings of closeness and warmth to a child. Pets always have the time to play with a child when parents and peers are unavailable. When you have scolded your child, the family pet will still be there (wagging its tail, purring or otherwise making itself available for affection) to remind your child that he or she is still loved.

Children who grow up with pets share many good qualities. Pets can offer examples of good behavior for children. As you train and discipline your pet, your child will begin to understand that there are limits of acceptable behavior. Often, children with pets are kinder and more considerate of both animals and other children. Adolescents who live with a pet often have higher self-esteem than their peers who have never loved and cared for an animal.

As children grow to be toddlers and beyond, they can help in the feeding, watering, walking and grooming of the family pet. Participating in the care of your pet will give your children a sense of responsibility and the satisfaction of caring for another living being.

Children with pets learn to understand and respect animals. Just watching a family pet can teach a very young child in a simple way about the differences between animals and people. A child can learn how an animal functions within a family unit and about what a pet can and cannot contribute to the household. Observing a pet go through its life cycle (maturation, the birth of young, old age and death) can help a child to understand and accept the stages of life.

The lessons learned with the family pet can aid your child when he or she encounters an unfamiliar animal. A youngster who is raised with a pet is less likely to be frightened. In addition, a child who knows not to tease or harm an animal will probably act properly around a strange dog or cat. Showing little fear and taking proper action can significantly reduce the risk of your child being injured from such an encounter.

The benefits derived by your child may take on added value if he or she is the only youngster in the household. The interaction with a dog and cat could have some of the same benefits as a relationship with a sibling. It is even possible that an "only child" may consider the family pet to be a peer as well as a companion.

Having a pet may be particularly advantageous for a shy or withdrawn child. Many children respond better to animals than to people (other than their parents) in the early stages of life. A pet can be a supportive friend that a child can talk to. And in times of sadness or loss, the child may turn to the animal for solace.

The social benefits of pet ownership are often apparent. Pets help "break the ice" for your children. It is easy to socialize with an affectionate or playful animal. People often approach a playful dog and strike up a conversation with the owner.

Benefits For the Family

Besides the benefits to your child, pets can have a positive influence on the health of your entire family. Pet owners usually have fewer chronic illnesses and accidents. In addition, they frequently live longer than those who do not have pets. People with pets often have lower blood pressure and a higher survival rate after heart attacks than those who do not enjoy the companionship of an animal. It is not that the actual presence of an animal extends the life of the owner; it is the bond or attachment to the pet that can generate a special effect. This especially applies to those who live alone such as the elderly. Even a pet as simple as a goldfish can be beneficial; one study indicated that watching fish in an aquarium before dental surgery lowered blood pressure and had the same effect as hypnosis!

Some pets offer people an opportunity to exercise regularly. Walking a dog at least once a day can lead to some cardiovascular benefits. Playing with a dog can be as light or strenuous an exercise as you desire.

Dogs, large and small, also provide a measure of security. Besides reducing the chance of an intruder entering your home, a pet can be very protective of your child. Even the most gentle dog can become aggressive if it perceives that someone poses a threat to a loved one.

Regardless of the benefits of keeping a family pet, some people consider removing their pet from the household when their baby arrives. This alternative is neither pleasant nor optimistic. It is difficult to place an animal in a new home, especially if your pet is old or has health problems. Each year, approximately 12 to 15 million healthy dogs and cats are euthanized in shelters because new homes could not be found for them. With a little patience, understanding and effort, many of these deaths could be avoided. Given the opportunity, most pets could become best friends with your child.

Chapter Two
Normal Animal Behavior

To understand why a pet behaves as it does in your home, you need to be familiar with how it's wild ancestors functioned. Many of their innate behaviors are still present in your dog and cat after thousands of years of domestication. By studying these, you can learn how an animal "thinks" and what actions it may take in certain circumstances. Knowing this may enable you to predict its responses as well as give you better control over your animal. It will also help you safely build the relationship between your pet and your child.

Dogs

Dogs are social animals; they thrive in groups. Unfortunately, there is limited information on how dogs behave in the wild. However, many studies have been conducted on wolves, which are closely related to dogs.

Wolf packs are organized in loose hierarchies. There are an "alpha" male and female that are the leaders of the pack. The other animals align themselves behind the alpha animals. While this alignment is not a well-defined line of succession, there is a rough order. Every wolf knows its place within the group. This enables the wolves to live peacefully as a pack.

The "alpha" female is the only wolf that has puppies. All females in the pack assist in the care of the offspring. One of their responsibilities is to keep the sleeping area clean by licking the urine and feces from the puppies. Domestic dogs may also exhibit this caring trait. You may notice your female dog trying to eat soiled diapers. As disgusting as the act appears, your dog does not know that it is misbehaving; it is merely following its instincts.

Pack hierarchies are based on dominance. Wolves use certain signs of aggression and submission to establish and confirm their place in the pack. Once dominance is set, aggressive behavior tends to arise only when the structure of the pack is challenged. For a wolf to rise within the pack, it must challenge and dominate an animal in a higher position.

You can often read how your dog is reacting in a social situation by watching its behavior. When meeting other animals or people, dogs use body language and vocalization to signal dominance or submission. An aggressive, dominant dog may growl, bare its teeth, raise its hackles and bite. When it meets a submissive dog, the aggressor will assume a rigid body stance and may even try to mount the other animal. A submissive dog, on the other hand, may crouch towards the ground, roll over and possibly nuzzle the dominant dog's face.

From your dog's perspective, your family functions like a pack. The integrity of this group is important to your dog's well-being, both before and after the baby's arrival. The adults are the "alpha" animals with the children and the pets loosely structured in a hierarchy beneath them. Most canines instinctively mistrust outsiders attempting to join the pack. So when a new child comes home, your dog must learn that your baby is a cherished member of the group. In addition, because the new member requires a place in the hierarchy, you may need to teach your pet that the child has a higher position. The dog must be submissive and not challenge the child.

Another normal behavioral pattern is that most dogs will protect their food. Wild canines guard their food from other animals. This instinct affects domestic dogs as well. Even the most gentle dog may growl and act aggressively toward anyone who the dog perceives is stealing its food. Your dog should be taught at a young age not to react aggressively whenever its food is removed or touched. However, you should also teach each member of your family to maintain a respectful distance when the animal is eating its food or treats.

A third instinct that you may notice about your dog is that it will seek out a special place in your home to call its own. Dogs, by nature, are den animals. In the wild, the den is a place where a wolf can rest safely. It also serves as a nest in which the puppies are born and spend their early days. It is this nesting instinct that allows the animal to be house-broken. A dog will generally keep its den clean; it instinctively avoids soiling in its sleeping area. In addition, the dog's desire for a secure retreat will enable you to confine it when necessary. This will be important for the times when you cannot supervise your dog and child.

Cats

In contrast to dogs, cats are generally solitary creatures. Domestic cats developed from wild cats, which were not pack animals. A female cat raises her young without assistance from the male. Kittens stay with the mother for several months. After that period, they may disperse and establish their own home ranges.

If food is plentiful, cats may form a loose pack.

If you have more than one cat, your cats may play, eat and sleep together. They may even groom each other. Cats, however, do not develop a social hierarchy like dogs do.

When cats meet, you can determine their compatibility by their body language. If they are not compatible, you might see signs of aggression such as the hair standing up, the back arched, the ears pointed toward the other cat and the tail rigid or twitching. Cats may also "talk" when they are feeling aggressive.

While cats are solitary creatures, they do express and want affection. Many cats enjoy—and even demand—close physical contact such as holding, cuddling, petting or stroking. Other cats may love to be near you but may resist any attempt to be touched or picked up. Still others will shun most interactions of any sort. Each cat will decide how much contact it wants. Your pet's interactions with your new baby will depend on your cat's individual personality.

Once a cat has accepted a person, it will usually rub its face and body against that individual. This is an act of marking; the cat is using scent glands located near the mouth and the base of the tail to mark that person with the cat's scent. While the marking is too delicate for human senses, the cat can readily detect it and knows that all "friends" have a similar scent. Your cat, once it accepts the baby, will want to rub against and mark the child. This should not be considered aggressive behavior. Of course, even friendly interactions must be closely supervised.

A cat accepts the people in the household because it is taught, through handling as a kitten, that the owners are caregivers. As such, the owner is often viewed as a surrogate parent. Many adult cats still consider themselves kittens in their relationship with humans. You may notice this characteristic if your cat kneads its paws on your lap or on warm, soft objects, such as wool blankets. This behavior, coupled with purring, mimics the actions of a kitten attempting to get milk from its mother. If your pet likes to knead your lap, it may also attempt to perform this action on your child. Not allowing your cat to do this to your baby will prevent your child from being accidentally scratched.

Cats like warm, cozy places. Your baby's crib is just such a spot. Your pet may try to sleep on or near your child. Although you should not allow your cat to sleep in your child's crib, it is not for the reasons that are often cited. Many people believe that a cat can suck the life out of a baby by drawing out the infant's breath. This is myth based on a medieval superstition that cats were the feline manifestation of witches. It is also not true that cats smother babies by lying on the baby's face. Cats should be kept out of cribs because they can accidentally scratch or injure a young child.

People cannot dominate cats in the same way that they can dominate dogs. However, it is possible to exercise some control over your cat and have your cat respond to some of your commands. Cats can be trained to sit and come when called. Some cats will even do tricks such as meowing on command, fetching and playing games.

An example of the different natures of cats and dogs occurs when they are being annoyed by a child. Many toddlers delight in pulling an animal's tail. A cat is likely to run off at the first sight of the child; it would rather be left alone and in peace. A dog, on the other hand, is a more social creature. It would rather be in the company of its pack than be alone. A dog may let the child tease it until the dog is past the point of tolerance. Then it may react aggressively towards the child.

That is not to say that a cat may not be dangerous. A cat may be upset about receiving less attention since the baby arrived; a child's teasing can anger the cat. If it feels that the child is a threat, the cat may scratch or bite. An injury caused by a cat can be just as devastating as that caused by a dog. Any wound can become infected and scar. Being injured can also lead to emotional trauma. The chance of your child sustaining an injury can be drastically reduced if all interactions between your child and any animal are closely supervised.

Educating Yourself About Your Pet

While the behavioral patterns discussed in this chapter apply to most dogs and cats, they do not apply to all. Every breed is different. Even individuals within breeds have different tendencies. For instance, many families get retrievers because of their reputation for gentleness and shun terriers because of their tendency to be very active. However, there are retrievers that are aggressive and terriers that are docile.

You should take the time to understand what makes your pet behave as it does. By doing so, you can determine your individual dog's or cat's normal behavior pattern. You may then be able to notice if the animal undergoes any unusual behavioral changes after the baby arrives. They could be the first sign of trouble if a problem begins to develop. You can learn about your pet by asking yourself a number of questions.

• Although responsive and gentle to you, has your pet ever threatened others?

- Have jealous-like tendencies in your pet ever resulted in physical attacks?
- When previously exposed to infants or children, did your pet react by taking an aggressive posture? Did your dog growl or nip? Did your cat scratch or bite?

If the answer to any of these questions is "yes", think about the circumstances in which your pet acted in an aggressive manner.

- Was your pet in pain or frightened when it growled, scratched or bit?
- Was your pet being teased or playing rough when the incidents occured?
- Was someone handling your pet's puppies, kittens, food or favorite toy when it acted aggressively?
- Was your pet in a sexually active phase when the events took place?
- Has your pet ever shown aggressive tendencies without provocation?

If past episodes of aggression were caused by specific behaviors or circumstances, you may have a problem that can be easily corrected. Once the situations that triggered the responses are eliminated, the aggressive behavior should disappear. For instance, a pet may react aggressively to any touch or manipulation if it is in pain or recovering from an injury. Once the pain is gone, the animal probably will not respond forcefully to normal attention. On the other hand, if your pet has attacked another person or you without provocation, you have a serious problem. You should discuss the situation with your veterinarian, a trainer or an animal behavior specialist.

Predatory behavior is a normal instinct in domestic dogs and cats. Their ancestors hunted for food; your pet will probably exhibit the same trait. Most animals that hunt can co-exist in harmony with children. If your pet has killed another animal, you should think about the circumstances under which the killing took place.

- Did your pet hunt and kill an animal such as a mouse, bird or squirrel for food?
- Did your pet kill another animal only as an act of aggression?

If your pet hunted and killed a small animal for food, your pet may be fine with children. Often, for example, cats will bring home "gifts" of small birds or mice that they have killed for their owners. This is a sign of affection by the cat and does not indicate that it is dangerously aggressive. A dog may also kill a small animal for food. If the kill is not eaten right away, it may be saved for a time when your dog is hungry.

Although a rare occurence, it is possible that

your pet will mistake your baby for a prey animal. A newborn child is small and helpless. He or she is not mobile and will flail the arms and legs. To an animal, these are the same traits that are often exhibited by its prey. You should carefully monitor your pet for signs of hunting during the baby's first several weeks. This is when your newborn will be most vulnerable and prey-like. To help ward off this behavior, your pet may benefit from prior exposure to infants and small children. Once your pet has accepted the child as a member of the family, the danger will probably subside.

However, if you notice that your pet has a fixed, constant stare trained on your baby or displays other signs of hunting, your infant is in peril. Do not underestimate the danger. You must act at once and protect the baby. The animal should be sternly corrected. You should also seek professional help to remedy the situation. Until you are confident that the animal will pose no threat to your child, the dog must be kept separated from the child.

You may also have a problem if your pet has killed another animal in a fight over territory, dominance or food. Even if your dog or cat accepts your child as a member of the family, it can be a threat to the baby. As your child grows, he or she will undoubtedly place your pet in a position where the animal feels threatened. If the animal has a history of fighting, it may respond in a similar fashion again. Consult your pet care professional about your specific situation.

Guard dogs can be excellent family pets and very gentle with children. However, any animal used to guard your home and family should be professionally trained. A properly trained dog will attack only when commanded to do so and is taught to hold its targets, not bite them. Thus, it is unlikely that such a dog would attack a child. However, it can happen. Even well-trained guard dogs have lapses. Since their aggressive behavior has been reinforced, they are more likely to respond forcefully in a particular situation than a dog that has not been trained for protection.

On the other hand, an improperly trained guard dog is always a dangerous animal. Often, a dog that has been encouraged to be vicious is aggressive as the result of being abused. Its aggression comes from fear. Any time that an animal such as this is scared, it may attack. It cannot be trusted around adults or children.

Many dogs show aggression when people such as letter carriers and delivery personnel come to your door. Your dog may rush towards the door in a ferocious manner. While a dog "attacking" the "intruder" will probably not intentionally harm your child, your child may be injured if he or she happens to be in the way as the dog approaches the door. Proper supervision should enable you to avoid such a circumstance.

Chapter Three
Good Health Care

The first aspect of preparing your dog or cat for the arrival of your child deals with your pet's health care. The good health of your animal is critical, not only for your pet, but also for your entire family. There are diseases and viruses that an animal can transmit to human beings. (This chapter briefly covers these diseases. An expanded discussion can be found in Appendix B: Zoonotic Diseases.) In addition, an animal that is not healthy will not be as accepting of the changes and stresses brought by a new addition to the family. To check and maintain your pet's good health, you should take a number of steps.

Visiting Your Veterinarian

You should plan to make a pre-baby trip to your veterinarian. Discuss the pregnancy; there may be some special precautions that can help avoid prenatal complications. In addition, your veterinarian will check to see if your pet's innoculations are up-to-date, test for internal parasites and evaluate the overall well-being of your dog or cat. If your pet has not been neutered, you should consider that possibility. Although the following may appear to be extensive, most of these issues can be handled in one or two visits.

Vaccinations

Vaccines support your pet's immune system, the natural line of defense against disease. Regular vaccinations are needed in order for the immune system to remain strong. While most of the diseases prevented by vaccinations cannot be transmitted to human beings, you should still protect your pet from infection. A sick animal will not act normally around children. A dog or cat that is ill will be less tolerant and may become more aggressive than it ordinarily would be.

Dogs and cats receive different sets of vaccinations. Your dog should receive a series of five inoculations over the course of a few weeks:

- Rabies
- DHLP (distemper, hepatitis, leptospirosis, parainfluenza)
- Bordatella (also known as kennel cough)
- Parvo virus
- Corona virus

There is also a new vaccine that protects against Lyme disease. Your veterinarian may recommend that your dog receive this inoculation as well.

A cat needs three inoculations:

- Rabies
- Upper respiratory disease complex, which
  includes one or more of the following:
  feline distemper, calici virus,
  rhinotracheitis and chlamydia
- Feline leukemia virus

There is also a new vaccine against feline infectious peritonitis that your veterinarian may recommend.

The one vaccination that the two animals have in common is rabies. Rabies is a viral disease that attacks the nervous system of mammals. It is lethal to both animals and human beings who contract it. Rabies is spread through saliva transmitted via bites. Although wild animals, such as raccoons, are the principal carriers, domestic animals can carry the disease.

If your pet has a current rabies vaccination, it cannot contract rabies or carry the virus. This means that your pet cannot transfer rabies to any person, even if the pet is bitten by a rabid animal. A dog or cat that is correctly vaccinated will only need a booster shot to strengthen the immune system. But an unvaccinated pet that is bitten is a threat to your child. It will need to be quarantined for several months or destroyed.

Because dogs and cats can carry rabies, most

communities have ordinances requiring that all domestic pets be vaccinated against the virus. The inoculation procedures differ from location to location; you should consult your veterinarian for the procedures in your area. All young dogs and cats receive a vaccination that lasts for one year. After this shot, the time interval between inoculations may be one, two or three years, depending on where you live and the type of vaccine. It is important that you know when to re-vaccinate your pet; your veterinarian should give you a certificate of vaccination indicating how long it lasts.

Internal Parasites

In addition to bringing your pet up-to-date with its vaccinations, your veterinarian will check your dog or cat for internal parasites. The most common of these are listed below.

- Roundworm
- Tapeworm
- Hookworm
- Whipworm (dogs only)
- Coccidia
- Giardia
- Toxoplasma (cats only)

Animals usually contract internal parasites by ingesting the parasite itself. This occurs by eating infected animals (such as a mouse or a bird), swallowing an infected flea, eating contaminated fecal material or drinking contaminated water. Most parasites affect the digestive system and lead to problems such as vomiting, diarrhea and weight loss. Some of these parasites can be transmitted to human beings. If they infect a child, they may lead to a serious illness.

To test for internal parasites, your veterinarian will need a fresh sample of your pet's feces, also known as a stool sample. This sample should be less than twelve hours old and should be refrigerated until you deliver it to your veterinarian.

Most pets with internal parasites can be treated easily. Your veterinarian will give your dog or cat an injection and/or oral medication. This treatment is usually accomplished in more than one stage. The first set kills the existing adult parasites but not the immature forms. The second kills the young parasites after they have hatched and before they have time to lay new eggs.

Some of the parasites that infect animals can be transmitted to human beings. It is critical that pregnant women be aware of the dangers of toxoplasmosis. The parasite that causes toxoplasmosis is transmitted by eating raw or undercooked meat that is infected or by ingesting the parasite after accidentally touching cat feces. Most people do not experience any symptoms or require treatment for the infection. However, if a woman contracts toxoplasmosis during pregnancy, it can harm the unborn child.

Toxoplasmosis can be easily prevented. Avoid raw or undercooked meat, particularly pork and mutton. Also, change the litter box daily to eliminate the parasite before it becomes infective. This job should not be the responsibility of the pregnant woman; someone else should perform this task. However, if an expectant mother must clean the box, she should avoid contact with the cat feces; she should wear gloves and wash her hands thoroughly afterwards. In addition, a pregnant woman should wear gloves if she is working in the garden to avoid exposure to fecal material; again, the hands should be thoroughly washed afterwards.

Your cat can easily be tested for the organism. It is done with a simple blood test. If the test is negative and your cat does not go outside your home, it cannot contract toxoplasmosis (unless it eats raw or undercooked meat that is infected). Although the possibility of contracting toxoplasmosis by touching a cat is minimal, contact with other people's felines should be limited to indoor cats that are not fed raw meat.

If your cat does have the organism and you were exposed before becoming pregnant, there is probably no cause for alarm. Problems with the fetus arise only when the disease is contracted during pregnancy. Your health care professional is in the best position to answer your questions and concerns about toxoplasmosis.

Although it is rare, your family can also contract roundworms from your pet. Most puppies and kittens are infected with the parasite. Among the symptoms are swelling of the belly, diarrhea and weight loss. Your veterinarian will test your dog or cat for roundworms at its regular visit. All puppies and kittens should be routinely treated. If your pet has a distended belly or other symptoms of digestive tract disease, you should take it to the veterinarian.

Children cannot get roundworms directly from an animal. The worms are transmitted to animals and humans through feces. When a dog or cat is infected with the parasite, it will pass roundworm eggs in its feces. After 10 to 14 days in dirt or grass, the eggs become infective. Children may inadvertently ingest the tiny roundworm eggs if they swallow contaminated dirt.

Roundworm infection in children is treatable, but it is relatively easy to prevent. First, identify and treat intestinal worms in your pet. Second, because the eggs must sit for approximately two weeks before they become infective, you should clean up your pet's feces promptly. Last, you should instruct your children to keep their hands out of their mouths and to wash up after playing in the yard or garden.

External Parasites

In addition to checking for internal parasites,

your veterinarian will check for external parasites. These include fleas, ticks, mites, lice and ringworm. They often cause skin damage and make your pet irritable. An irritable pet may be less patient with your children. In addition, some external parasites can afflict your children as well.

Fleas

Fleas are one of the most common parasites. A single flea can cause havoc in your house. It can actually live for up to one year and can bite your pet repeatedly. If your dog or cat is allergic to flea bites, one bite will trigger constant scratching that may lead to skin infections.

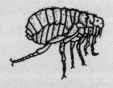

After a flea has fed, it will begin to lay eggs. A single flea can produce over 400 eggs in its lifetime. The eggs are laid on your pet but they can roll off onto the carpet, in between the floor boards or into any other place in your house or yard where the animal has been. The eggs hatch in about one or two weeks; the fleas mature into egg-laying adults in less than three weeks. As the offspring begin to reproduce, your flea population explodes. Adult fleas will bite and feed on all mammals in the household; this includes your pet, your family and you. The biting fleas can cause itchy sores on your child's skin.

Your veterinarian will help you decide the best plan to eradicate your flea problem. You must remember that you will have to treat both your pet and its environment. Also bear in mind that if there is a pregnant woman or small children in the house, you should limit the use of certain insecticides and chemicals. Check with your health care professional to determine which products are safe for your household.

The most common methods for treating a pet are medicated baths, dips, sprays, powders and flea collars. If you use chemical methods to treat your dog or cat for fleas, you should select the proper products, read the labels carefully and watch your pet for any adverse reaction. In addition, you should monitor your pet's interaction with your family. Close and repeated contact can be potentially dangerous for a child and even an adult. If any members of your family appear to become ill due to overexposure to a flea product, you should immediately contact your physician. You might want to isolate your pet from the family for a few days if it is being treated with a potent insecticide.

There are safer alternatives to insecticides that do not involve chemicals. These methods are milder but often less effective at killing fleas. By combining milder methods with insecticides, you may be able to reduce your family's and your pet's exposure to insecticides and still achieve adequate flea control.

Alternatives include dessicant powders, flea combs, food additives and ultrasonic collars. Dessicant powders are applied to the animal's coat and work by drying up and killing fleas. Flea combs are fine-toothed combs that grab the fleas as you comb your pet.

There are a few controversial options. Some people advocate feeding brewer's yeast, sulphur compounds or garlic. By ingesting these items, some of the product will eventually get into the animal's skin and supposedly produce a flea-repelling odor. Before using any of these dietary remedies, you should consult your veterinarian.

Another controversial product is a collar that emits a high frequency sound that some people believe repels fleas. You will not be able to hear the sound; however, your pet will. If you notice that the animal is acting strangely or experiencing any discomfort, you should discontinue use of this collar.

You must also treat your pet's environment. One of the best and safest methods is to vacuum your entire house frequently and thoroughly. This will remove fleas hiding in carpets, between the floorboards and on the furniture. Throw away the vacuum bag after each use and replace it with a new one. Otherwise, the flea eggs will hatch in the warm, cozy interior of the bag.

If your house or yard is heavily infested with fleas, you may need to take more drastic measures. One option is to use a flea "bomb" or "fogger"; these are aerosolized insecticides designed to kill fleas and their larvae. These are very effective; some products even have a residual effect that will kill hatching fleas for months.

These products are also dangerous if improperly used. As with the products used to treat your pet, you should read all labels and carefully follow all directions, paying particular attention to all cautions and warnings. Be sure to check with your physician before using such a product if a member of your household is pregnant or if there are small children around. Specific questions regarding a pesticide can be answered by contacting the manufacturer or calling your veterinarian.

If the dangers of a particular treatment appear to be too great, your physician or your veterinarian may be able to recommend an alternative. One environmental alternative is the use of non-toxic dessicants, such as diatomaceous earth or silica; these are sprinkled on floors and rugs. Cedar chips, another alternative, can be used in your pet's bedding; they are a natural flea repellant. They will not kill the fleas but they do repel them. By treating the environment as well as the pet, you can prevent flea bites on your pet and child.

Ticks

Ticks are another external parasite that are common among pets. A tick will bite, attach itself and feed on the blood of almost any animal; this includes humans as well as dogs and cats. The danger is that a tick may inject a disease-causing organism when the tick attaches itself to the host to feed. The most well-known of these diseases are Rocky Mountain spotted fever and Lyme disease.

The most effective products for tick control are chemicals and insecticides similar to those used to kill fleas. Many are available to fit your particular needs. However, before using any pesticide or chemical, you should consult your health care professional about the dangers posed to pregnant women and children.

Tick season occurs during warm weather. During this time, you should check your pet every day for ticks. If you find one on your dog or cat, you should remove it immediately. Prompt action prevents the tick from having enough time to inject disease-causing organisms.

To remove an embedded tick, use tweezers to grasp the tick at the point where it is attached to the animal. Use a steady motion to pull it off. Do not try to "drown" the tick with a chemical or to burn it while it is still attached to your pet.

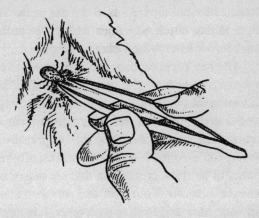

After removing the tick, do not squash it with your hand. You can kill it by drowning it in alcohol. Afterwards, discard the tick. However, if your child has been bitten by a tick, call your pediatrician before killing and discarding the parasite. Your doctor may want to see and test it for infective organisms. Seal the tick in a plastic bag or a clean jar. It will suffocate but it will be preserved for testing.

Other external animal parasites such as mites and lice are not generally a problem for children or babies; these parasites survive for a only a short period of time off the host animal. As a result, their infestation of people is self-limiting and clears itself.

However, they can lead to skin diseases on your dog or cat. They will make your pet uncomfortable and will make it less patient with a child. You should eliminate these parasites from your pet as soon as they are detected. This is accomplished by the use of special baths and dips. As with the use of flea and tick products, check with your health care professional before employing a bath or a dip.

Another parasite that can infect humans is ringworm. In reality, the name "ringworm" is a misnomer; the parasite is not a worm. It is a fungus that sits under the skin. Its name comes from the circular skin lesions caused by the fungus when it infects people. Animals with ringworm usually have patches of hairless, crusty skin that are one or two inches in diameter. Your child and pet can transmit ringworm back and forth to each other. It is treated in both humans and animals by a combination of ointments, shampoos and oral medications. If you suspect that your pet has ringworm, take it to your veterinarian immediately; quick action may prevent having to treat your family as well.

Additional Procedures

In addition to the basic procedures that should be performed annually, there are a couple of surgical procedures that could have an impact on the relationship between your pet and your child. They are discussed below.

Neutering

If your pet has not been neutered, you should discuss this procedure with your veterinarian. Neutering is the removal of the reproductive organs of a male or female. For a male, this operation is known as altering or castrating; spaying refers to that for a female.

A popular misconception is that neutering your dog or cat will drastically change your pet. This is untrue. Altering a male or spaying a female will probably affect its behavior slightly but it will not change its basic personality or temperament. Especially with a new baby on the way, the advantages of altering your pet outweigh the disadvantages.

Male dogs that have not been neutered tend to roam more and to be more aggressive to other dogs and people. These dogs may frequently mark their territory by depositing small amounts of urine in several locations; they can become very protective of that territory. They are harder to train and to control if there is a female dog in heat within scenting distance. From a medical standpoint, they are more likely to have trouble with their prostate gland later in life.

Just like male dogs, male cats should be neutered. Altered male cats do not roam, fight or "spray" urine indoors as much as cats that have not been neutered. They stay cleaner, are less territorial and are less likely to become injured by fighting with other cats.

One obvious advantage of spaying your female pet is preventing an unwanted pregnancy. With a new baby in the house, life will be exciting and challenging enough without the added burden of a litter of puppies or kittens. Other advantages exist as well. Your pet's temperament will be calmer and more stable without the hormonal fluctuations that accompany the reproductive cycle. Also, female dogs neutered before their first heat do not develop cancer of the mammary glands later in life.

Unspayed female dogs and cats go into heat. At this time, they are receptive and attractive to males. When unaltered males pick up the scent of your female, they will come calling. It is not unusual for male dogs to fight each other when approaching a receptive female. Your child could be seriously injured if he or she were to accidently get caught between the males and the female.

Even if your female dog completes her cycle without becoming pregnant, she will begin to act as if she is. This is known as a false pregnancy. She may begin to build a nest and to "mother" toys and other objects. The act of becoming more protective and aggressive at this time may pose a threat to your child.

Some people are hesitant to spay a female dog or cat before she has had offspring. They believe that a female will be unhappy or unfulfilled if she is not allowed to have at least one litter. However, you should not attribute human feelings to animals. There is no evidence that female animals that have never given birth are less happy or fulfilled than those that have had a litter.

Some parents want their children to observe the miracle of childbirth firsthand by watching their pet have a litter. While this may be an educational experience for children, many puppies and kittens cannot be placed in permanent homes. Each year, over 12 million animals are "put to sleep" because their owners were unable or unwilling to care for them any longer. Allowing your female to have a litter may add to that sad number.

Declawing

Another optional procedure to discuss with your veterinarian applies to cats. This is declawing. It is having the last bone and nail surgically removed from each of the front toes. Once they are gone, they will not grow back.

This procedure is not recommended for a number of reasons. First, the bones and nails in the paws assist the cat in balancing. Removing them may affect its coordination and its ability to jump. Second, a cat without front claws will have a difficult time defending itself. It cannot swipe at an adversary or escape a predator by climbing a tree. Third, the claws probably will not pose a threat to your child. A cat is more likely to run away than to fight when it is being bothered by a child. Most cats will attack only as a last resort. Last, the procedure may not make your child's environment safer. The cat will probably have its back claws. If your child annoys your pet, the cat may grab your child's arm with its front feet and rake the arm with its hind claws. A lack of front claws may also result in a cat that bites. Declawing is not the solution that will diminish the threat to your child posed by an aggresssive cat.

However, if you feel that your only alternatives are declawing the cat or removing it from the household, the most humane solution is having the claws taken out. Most cats given to shelters are not placed in new homes; more often, they are eventually destroyed. Consider your options carefully.

Chapter Four
Grooming

Grooming is critical for all pets. Good grooming techniques will enable you to monitor your pet's health between visits to your veterinarian. A clean, healthy animal will be a better pet for your child.

Benefits of Regular Grooming

A thorough grooming regimen has a number of benefits. First, it is one of the keys to the maintenance of your pet's good health. As you groom your pet, you should check its entire body. While you may not be able to diagnose an illness, you will be able to notice a change from its normal condition. Early detection and treatment can prevent a disease or a parasite infestation from becoming serious.

Maintaining your pet's good health is critical for your entire family. Early detection of a deviation in your dog's or cat's normal condition may prevent a parasite or illness from being transmitted to another member of your family. In addition, a dog or cat that is not feeling well or is in pain is more likely to respond aggressively to a child who wants to play.

Another benefit of grooming is that animals enjoy it. Most pets like the attention from their owners. Regular grooming will solidify the bond between your pet and you. As your child matures, you can allow him or her to participate in and even be responsible for some aspects of your pet's health maintenance program. This will help build a strong relationship between them.

An additional benefit is that regular grooming will accustom your pet to being touched and manipulated. This will reduce the danger for your youngster. If your pet becomes used to being handled, it will be less likely to respond aggressively to the attentions of a child.

Brushing the Coat

Daily brushing or combing of your pet's coat will help keep it clean, glossy and free of mats. In addition, it will enable you to closely examine your dog's or cat's skin. Over a period of time, you will learn its normal condition. This will enable you to recognize any changes that may signal a health problem.

Daily grooming of the coat will also prevent the hair from becoming matted or knotted. This is especially crucial for long-haired animals. A matted coat may cause your pet to scratch. Excessive scratching can lead to open sores and possible infection.

Even though a cat often grooms itself, you should brush its coat regularly. Thorough brushing will accustom your cat to being handled and remove excess hair. Its removal will prevent your cat from swallowing it, thus reducing the chance of hairballs forming in the digestive system.

Checking the Ears

As with the skin, periodic examinations of your pet's ears will allow you to determine their normal condition. When checking the ears, you should pay careful attention to the ear canal and flap. Any change, such as unusual odor, discharge or redness, signals trouble and warrants a visit to your veterinarian.

A healthy ear has a safety benefit for your child. While you should teach your child not to tug on your pet's ears, he or she may do it anyway. If there is an infection, this pulling will be painful for the animal and may lead to an aggressive response.

Checking the Eyes

Your pet's eyes should be clear and bright, held open without squinting and have a minimum of discharge. Some pets, especially those with flat faces, have a slight amount of clear tears constantly draining from their eyes. This is not to be confused with heavy, clouded or colored discharge from the eyes, which signals disease. Other warning signs are eyes that are cloudy, red or closed. All pets with eye trouble should be seen immediately by your veterinarian. Eye disease that is not treated quickly can lead to loss of sight.

Injured, inflamed or infected eyes are painful. A pet with an eye problem may respond forcefully if your child should try to touch its face. In addition, an eye problem may obscure your pet's sight. An animal with poor vision is more easily upset and frightened by changes in its immediate environment. Your child's actions could be misinterpreted by your pet and could lead to an adverse response.

Checking the Mouth

An examination of the mouth consists of checking the condition of the teeth, gums, tongue and lips. The teeth should be relatively white and free of deposits of plaque or tartar. The tongue, gums and lips of most pets are a shade of pale pink. Some pets, however, have black pigment in parts of their mouths.

This is normal coloration and should not be confused with plaque, tartar or a disease process.

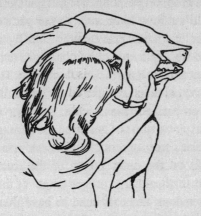

For a dog, you can take steps each day to help it maintain healthy teeth and gums. Giving your dog treats like biscuits can clean the teeth and stimulate the gums. Chewing on toys like rawhide and nylon bones can also be beneficial to your dog. In addition, many veterinarians recommend that you brush your dog's teeth. If you do, you should not use a toothbrush and paste designed for humans. Many products that meet the specific needs of a dog are available.

Your veterinarian may show you how to scrape tartar off your pet's teeth at home. This can be helpful but it will not replace brushing the animal's teeth. Despite all your efforts, your pet may need to have its teeth cleaned by your veterinarian periodically.

Your Pet's Nails

One grooming task has a significant impact on your child's safety. Maintaining your pet's nails at the proper length may prevent your child from being scratched while playing with your dog or cat. Some pets do not need to have their nails clipped. The nails of many active dogs are filed down by running and walking on hard surfaces such as driveways, sidewalks and playgrounds. Cats often use items such as rough fabrics, trees or scratching posts to remove the dead cells on the outer sheath of the nails. This maintains the health and proper length of the nails.

Other dogs and cats need to have their nails clipped every few weeks. Older and less active animals as well as those that spend most of their time indoors are likely candidates. For these pets, you should check the nails to see if they have grown too long. If so, your veterinarian or a groomer can clip them. Or you can learn to do the task yourself.

If your pet has never had its nails cut, you should take a few steps before actually clipping them. For a few days, you should handle each of your pet's paws. Next, you should touch the tip of each nail with the clippers. After your dog or cat has become accustomed to having its paws manipulated and is used to the clippers, you can clip the nails.

When clipping the nail of a dog or cat, you should take care not to hit the quick. The quick is the vein that runs partway down the nail and supplies it with blood. It is the pink area just beneath the surface of the nail.

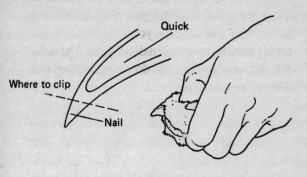

If you do cut the quick, the nail will bleed. If this happens, you may be able to stop the bleeding by applying a clotting agent (available at most pet stores), putting pressure on the wound or pushing the nail into a bar of soap. If the bleeding does not stop within 5 minutes, you should contact your veterinarian.

Clipping a Dog's Nails

The proper length for a dog's nails is for the tips to be just above ground level as the animal stands. If the nails touch the ground, they force the toes to spread. This causes the dog to walk incorrectly and can eventually lead to foot deformities.

If your dog has white nails, you should be able to see the quick. You should be careful not to cut it when you clip the nail. If your dog has black nails, clip only the tip of the nail. This should allow you to avoid the quick. Use clippers designed for a dog's nails. Nail clippers designed for people are not strong enough for a dog's tough nails. After clipping the nail, you may need to smooth the nail by filing it with an emery board.

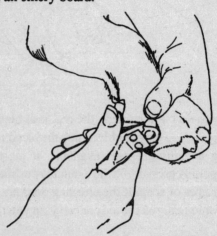

In addition, be sure to check the nail of the dewclaw. This is the claw that is on the inside of the legs. If it is not periodically trimmed, it can circle back on itself and cut into the dog's leg.

Clipping a Cat's Nails

A cat's nails need to be clipped if they start to

turn back on themselves or if they constantly get stuck on furniture and carpet. To trim a cat's nails, you must first push each toe from beneath the pad to fully extend the nail. Once this is done, you should clip the end of each nail, taking care not to hit the quick. You can use either your own clippers or one designed for animals. The nail of a cat probably will not need to be filed smooth after clipping.

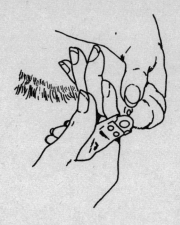

Chapter Five
Obedience Training and Adjusting Routines

A crucial step in preparing your pet for the arrival of your child is obedience training. You must be confident that your pet will respond to your commands immediately and consistently. Proper training takes time and patience. However, the effort will pay off. You will have the satisfaction of knowing that you can exercise better control over your pet. And your pet will be calmer and happier because it will have a clear sense of its own limits and know what you expect from it.

The Crate—A Dog's Den

A crate is an invaluable investment for a dog owner expecting a baby. The crate serves many functions. It gives a dog a secure place within the house where it can rest and sleep; in this fashion, your dog will consider the crate to be its den. With the knowledge that a dog will not soil its den, you can use the crate to help housebreak a puppy. In addition, confining a puppy to a crate while you are away will prevent the destruction of such things as shoes or furniture. If your dog is used to a crate, travelling by car, plane or train will be easier. Most important, a crate offers a place where you can restrain the dog or where it can seek refuge from the unwanted attention of a child.

There are two basic types of crates; the one that you use depends on your preferences and needs. A hard-sided crate is usually made of heavy plastic with large holes in the side. The door is wire mesh. This resembles a dog's den where all sides are enclosed with the exception of the opening used as an entrance. Airlines generally require this type of crate for transporting a dog.

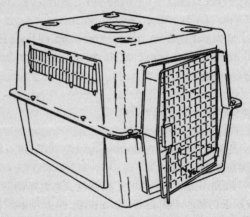

A show crate is one made entirely of wire with a metal sheet that can be slid in to serve as the floor. Most of these crates can be disassembled or folded flat for easy storage and transportation. Since all sides are exposed, you may want to place a blanket or a specially designed crate cover over it. However, the opening should always be exposed. This will simulate the environment of a den.

Whichever type of crate you choose, your dog should be able to stand up, lie down and turn around in the crate without struggling. And there should still be room for a water dish and perhaps a food dish. The crate should be near your family's activity areas. With this, your dog will be less likely to consider the crate as punishment and may seek out the crate on its own when tired.

Puppies and young dogs accept crates quickly. An older dog will adapt to a crate over time. You may need to use food to coax the dog inside for the first few weeks. As long as the animal associates the crate with positive events, it will eventually become your dog's haven and special place. The crate should never be an instrument of punishment. If it were, it would be similar to a jail. The result would be that your dog rejects the crate as a den and struggles every time that you attempt to confine it.

Whether your animal is young or old, you should never keep it in a crate for long periods of time. Do not use it to hold your pet while you are at work. Although a dog will be content there for several hours, it will not be comfortable for seven or eight hours or longer. A canine in the wild would not spend such long periods of time in its den without getting up and moving about. You cannot expect a domestic dog to behave differently. If you must leave your dog in its crate for that much time, perhaps you can find someone to let it out for a brief period of exercise during the day.

Not all dogs will adapt to a crate. You may need to consider other options for those periods when you want to separate the dog from the rest of the family. A doghouse outside may be a solution. However, most dogs do not adapt well to being left outside for long periods of time.

Another solution is confining the animal to one room of the house, where it has a special blanket and favorite toys. Do not close the door if you do confine the dog to a single room. A dog shut up in one area will feel trapped and anxious; it will probably struggle to get out. The result will be an unhappy dog and a scratched door. A baby gate is just as useful at keeping a dog in one room as it can be in keeping a dog out of another. The dog can still see, smell and hear outside of the room and will be less anxious.

Training a Dog

Obedience training is the key to communicating with your dog. Once it is trained, your pet will no longer have to guess your intentions based solely on the tone of your voice. Instead, it will be able to relate your spoken word to the action that you require of it. Because they want to please their owners, most dogs respond quickly and enthusiastically to training. Your dog will see it as an opportunity for special attention from you; you should treat it in the same manner.

It is important that you train your dog before your child's arrival. This way the dog will have few distractions and plenty of time to learn and use his lessons. The longer that it has to practice, the better it will perform its obedience tasks. It will be more difficult to train your dog after the baby's birth. You will be more tired and have less patience for the dog. You will also have the baby to worry about. The best results will occur if you start obedience training well in advance.

You can learn how to train your dog by reading one or more of the many books that are available. If you prefer, enroll your dog in an obedience class. Many local organizations, such as humane societies, animal shelters, community colleges and recreational associations, offer classes at various levels. Individualized attention can be obtained by contacting a professional trainer. Your veterinarian can help you find a course suited to your needs.

Obedience classes are geared to dogs' ages and the levels of previous training. Upon completing a course, your dog should know the basics: "no", "heel", "come", "sit", "stay" and "down". Many trainers will include discussions of basic health care, housetraining, neutering your dog and overcoming behavioral problems such as barking or destructive chewing. There are puppy "kindergarten" classes and classes for adult dogs. No dog is too old or too dumb to be trained. Virtually all dogs and dog owners benefit from an obedience class of some sort.

You will need to practice with your pet every day, both during the course and afterwards. Frequent and consistent application of the commands is critical for success. If you do not practice or if you do not reinforce the commands in a consistent manner, your dog cannot be expected to respond in the correct manner. A few minutes of daily obedience exercises after completing training will help maintain your dog's skills. It will also keep the lines of communication open between your pet and you.

While many methods of training will get results, the best are those that utilize positive reinforcement. Praise, treats and affection work better than punishment. As you work with your dog, you should be firm but kind, calm and consistent. Harsh and brutal treatment is neither pleasant nor necessary. In addition, physical punishment does not always work. Often your pet learns to fear you and does not make the connection that its action led to the punishment.

Dogs learn by association. When training your pet to accept your child, it is crucial that you use positive reinforcement. Your dog should associate rewards and good feelings with your baby. Negative reinforcement will put the dog in a defensive position; as a result, your pet may associate your child with negative rather than positive feelings. For example, if you physically push your dog away every time it approaches the baby, the animal may connect the unpleasant act of being pushed with the presence of the child. On the other hand, a dog that receives praise when the baby is nearby will associate the pleasant response with the child.

One last point should be made about obedience training. Even a well-trained dog can have behavior problems if it has too much energy and too little exercise. In addition to a few minutes of daily training, it is also important to continue to provide adequate exercise for your dog after the baby arrives. A dog that gets plenty of exercise will be calmer and less likely to create problems.

Training a Cat

A cat is not as amenable as a dog to obedience training. A dog has a natural instinct to submit to a pack leader; a cat has a natural tendency to leave if it does not like the training session. If you decide to train your cat, keep the session short. Five minutes a day is usually enough.

However, a cat can be taught commands. By employing treats and praise, you can teach your cat to "come" when called. Use the same phrase and same tone of voice every time you call your cat. If you reward its cooperation by giving your cat a treat and plenty of affection, you will soon have a cat that comes on command. This can be useful if you need to call your cat away from your child.

Some negative behavior exhibited by your cat can be eliminated by startling the animal. (This works for dogs as well.) If you catch your pet in the act of misbehaving, you can stop it cold by startling it. Two effective methods are making a loud noise (such as rattling pebbles in a coffee can or using a bicycle horn) or squirting its hindquarters with a water pistol.

Water pistols work well with cats. For example, your cat may use your baby's playpen as a scratching post. If you yell at the cat, it simply learns to avoid the playpen when you are present. It knows that you are the source of its trouble and scratches only when you are not there. But if a stream of water comes from out of nowhere and interrupts the scratching, the cat will learn that clawing the playpen makes it wet and uncomfortable.

Three points need to be made about using a water pistol. First, the cat should not see you shoot the water pistol. If it does, it will learn not to misbehave in your presence but it may repeat its actions when you are not there. If the cat does not know that you are shooting it, the lesson learned is that its behavior led to the unpleasant outcome. Second, shoot only at the hindquarters; never aim at the face or head. Last, do not use any liquid other than water. Chemicals such as ammonia or other cleaning fluids can be extremely dangerous for an animal. The point is to startle the animal, not to blind or injure it.

When using a technique such as this to alter your pet's behavior, the key is consistency. You must use the same punishment every time the animal misbehaves. After a few times, your pet will associate the unpleasant feeling with the undesired action. Soon, it will cease that behavior. If your pet does not respond to this treatment in a relatively short time, you probably have a behavioral problem that requires professional help. You may want to consult your veterinarian or an animal behavior specialist.

Another strategy for altering a pet's behavior is to use a pet repellent. These chemicals were designed to be placed directly on furniture and other objects. Due to its unappealing taste or odor, it should prevent your pet from climbing on the furniture and from chewing or scratching objects of value. The problem is that your child will also have access to the furniture and objects sprayed with the repellent. You should read all labels and consult your child's health care professional before using any pet repellents in a place that may be accessible to your child. In addition, these repellents should not be used in a water gun. They are not designed to be placed on the animal directly.

Adjusting Routines

Animals are creatures of habit. They are happiest with a constant schedule of feedings, walks, playing and sleeping. Maintaining your pet's schedule and environment may help speed its adaptation to your baby. For instance, if you always walk your dog at 7:00 a.m. and then feed it afterwards, you should strive to continue that pattern once the baby arrives. If you cannot maintain your pet's schedule initially, you might ask someone else to do so or engage a pet-walking service until you can resume your normal activities.

However, if your pet's schedule or environment will be permanently altered once the baby arrives, you should make gradual changes in its routine as far in advance as possible. As soon as you know that the schedule will have to change, start the adjustment, even if the proposed plan seems out of place before the baby comes. This will allow for slow modification and give your pet the longest adjustment period.

For example, you feed your pet at night but plan to change the meal time to morning after the baby arrives. Begin the switch by giving the animal a small meal each morning. As you increase the size of the morning meal, you should slowly decrease the amount of food given in the evening. This change should be accomplished over several weeks and be established months before the baby's birth. When your child comes home, your pet will be accustomed to the change and will not associate it with the new arrival.

When planning a dog's or cat's daily schedule, make sure that you add play periods. Obedience training can be part, but not all, of this play time. Pets that have a specifically scheduled play period each day will be more tolerant of a decrease in attention following your baby's birth. Establish a daily play time for your pet before the child is born; maintain that time slot after the baby arrives.

Completing all adjustments to your pet's schedule and enviroment in advance will reduce the number of issues to tackle once your child comes home. The only changes to cope with will be those brought by the baby; those will be plenty!

Chapter Six
Educating Your Pet
About a Child

Before your baby is born, you can begin to educate your pet about children. By taking action before the baby arrives, you will pick up clues to how your dog or cat will react to having a new member of the family. This action may ease your pet's transition to its new position.

Introducing Your Pet To Other Children

If your pet has had limited exposure to children, introduce it to the children of your friends and neighbors. You may find that it is afraid of children; if so, controlled interaction with a child will help your pet overcome this fear. It will also give your pet a chance to discover the normal sights, sounds and smells of a child.

This introduction has added importance if your pet has strong predatory instincts. Some dogs may not recognize an infant as a human being. Given a baby's flailing limbs and high-pitched crying, a dog that has never encountered an infant may mistake the child for prey. This behavior would put your newborn in extreme danger. You can prevent the problem from developing by allowing your pet to becoming familiar with children before your baby is born. This will teach the animal two things. First, it will begin to understand that babies and toddlers are, in fact, people. Second, the dog will learn that aggressive behavior towards all youngsters is unacceptable.

The best method of introducing pets to children is to desensitize the animal. This is exposing a pet to various types, numbers and ages of children over a period of time. Gradually, your dog should become familiar with children and learn to act properly around them. It is imperative that you maintain calm but tight control over your dog whenever it is in the presence of children. An animal will be able to sense your mood. If you are nervous or anxious, you may make the dog excited. This will limit the success of the exercise.

The initial introduction should involve just your pet and one quiet, calm child. Place your dog in a sit/stay position. Praise the animal lavishly and reward its good behavior with a treat. Then allow the child to approach in a calm, confident manner. Continue to praise the dog. This initial meeting should last just until the animal begins to feel uncomfortable. You should stop the exposure before your pet misbehaves or if you sense that the dog is becoming tense.

Gradually increase the length of each meeting as the animal becomes used to the child. As the dog adjusts and relaxes, you should increase the number of children as well as the amount of physical contact and activity level. The goal is to acclimate the animal to a cross-section of children; as such, the additional children should vary in age and temperment. Soon, your pet should be able to handle a fairly large number of children engaged in a high level of activity without reacting aggressively.

Even if you are planning on having only one child, you should acclimate your pet to various groupings and ages of children. Your child and his or her playmates will go through different stages of development as they grow. Exposing your pet to these stages beforehand will reduce the chance of a problem cropping up.

There are three mistakes that you should avoid when desensitizing your pet to children. First, do not begin the acclimation process unless your dog has completed basic obedience training. If your dog has never been around children, you cannot predict what its reaction will be. Exposing a child to an untrained, unruly dog can be dangerous. You must be able to control your animal at all times.

Second, do not conduct the introductions in your house or yard. Your pet may perceive the children as threats and act to defend its territory. Your pet will be less likely to react in an aggressive manner away from your property. A better site would be a park or a neighbor's yard. After the animal has become accustomed to various numbers and types of youngsters, you can bring babies and children into your own home and yard.

The third mistake is to introduce too many children to your pet too soon. You cannot expect your animal to adapt well if you bombard it with new faces, sights and sounds. Moving too rapidly will overwhelm your pet; this could lead to an aggressive response towards the children. Your dog will then have to unlearn its negative impression about children before it can make progress towards accepting youngsters as friends. A gradual increase in the length of each exposure and the number of children introduced is the best approach. If you have any questions or doubts about your pet's ability to get along with children, consult your veterinarian or animal behavioral specialist.

A cat can be acclimated to children in much the same manner as a dog. It can be introduced initially to one child. Over time, the length of exposure and the number of children can be increased. Your cat is not likely to sit and stay on command. But you can restrain your pet with a harness and leash or by holding it on your lap during the introductions.

The Nursery

Once you have set up a nursery, you should let your pet explore it. There will be new and unusual furnishings that the animal will want to see and learn about. Allow your pet to examine these and other items that will be used by your baby, such as the stroller, carseat and backpack. However, you should not let your cat or dog mark (urinate in spots) the nursery or any of the baby's possessions. This is the manner by which an animal claims an area as its territory or range. The nursery should be the domain of your baby, not your pet.

If your pet will have access to the nursery, you should make sure that it cannot get into the diaper pail. As mentioned earlier, many dogs will attempt to eat soiled diapers. The plastic outer liners and fasteners of disposable diapers can become lodged in the dog's throat, stomach or intestines if ingested. The deodorizers and chemicals used to soak soiled cloth diapers may be poisonous. The best solution is to purchase a diaper pail whose lid fastens securely or to place the diaper pail in a closet.

One step that you can take to protect both your pet and your child is to make the nursery off limits to the animal. If you plan to do so, you should limit its access before the baby arrives. All changes in your pet's routine should be completed prior to the baby's coming home. If you give your pet free reign of the house now but reduce its range when the baby comes, your pet may associate the banishment with the child. You should avoid this negative association, if possible.

Block off the entrance in advance. You should use the same method of restriction both before and after the child arrives. Do not simply close the door. A closed door will keep your pet out of the nursery but it will also limit your ability to see and hear your baby. In addition, closed doors often have the effect of increasing your pet's curiosity. Animals that cannot tell what is behind a door may devise ways to get to the other side. If your pet can see into the baby's room, it will be less curious and less inclined to rush into the room every time that you open the door. If the door is to remain open after the baby arrives, it should be open before as well.

You should erect a barrier that will deny your pet access but still enable you to see and hear your baby. For a dog, a sturdy door gate may be sufficient. It should be high enough that the dog cannot jump over it. It should also be strong enough to withstand an attempt to knock it down. A variety of suitable gates are available. Be sure that the gate that you buy is easy to open and close, so that you will use it consistently.

Cats, being more agile than dogs, will require a more imposing barrier. One solution is to install a screen door. This may sound excessive but a screen door is very effective. First, by covering the entire opening, a screen door will prevent the cat from entering the nursery. Second, the screen enables you to see into the nursery and does not diminish your ability to hear your child. Last, it is easy to install and easier to use than a gate. With a screen door, you can quickly enter your baby's room without having to climb over a gate.

A barrier may be needed for your room as well. For the first few months, you may want your new baby to sleep in your bedroom. In that case, you may also want to restrict your pet's access to that area. If you plan to banish your pet from your room, do this before the baby arrives. It can be done by installing a gate or screen in your bedroom doorway, just like you did in the nursery.

If your dog or cat is allowed to enter the nursery, you should not let it jump into the crib. Most animals will not get into the crib. But if yours tries to, you might want to use a screen cover. Crib screens are designed to keep active babies from crawling out of their bed. Placing one of these over the crib will also keep a pet out. A screen will accomplish this without obstructing your view of your baby or your baby's view of the world.

Using the Senses

Animals have well developed senses. You can use them to help prepare your pet for the arrival of your child. Before the baby is born, you can begin to acclimate the animal to many of the sights, sounds and smells associated with a baby. You should involve your pet in baby-related activities. You might want to use a doll to play the part of "Baby". These exercises take only a few minutes and will help your pet adjust to the new activities associated with the infant. A few are listed below.

- Hold "Baby" in your arms or in a sling or backpack while going through your obedience training exercises.
- Pretend to change "Baby's" diapers while your dog sits and stays by your side. A curious cat would probably benefit from watching this as well.
- Push "Baby" in a stroller while walking the dog.

- Put "Baby" in a carseat and go for a ride with the dog.

You can use your pet's highly developed hearing to accustom it to the sounds that it will soon encounter. If you plan to play tapes of music in the nursery to soothe your baby, play the tapes for your pet to allow it to become familiarized with the sounds. You may even try playing a tape of a baby crying.

An animal's sense of smell is approximately 150 times more acute than that of a human being. You can use this to your advantage. Open the baby powder, oil, shampoo, ointments and other things that you will be using around your baby; let your pet smell them. Soiled diapers will smell of ammonia. Soak some diapers in ammonia, place them in the diaper pail and allow the animal to sniff them.

You should continue this training after the birth of your baby. Before you bring the infant home from the hospital, your pet should be allowed to sniff a blanket or outfit that has been in contact with the child. In this manner, your dog or cat will already recognize your baby's scent when your child arrives home.

Part II

AFTER
Your Child Arrives

Chapter Seven
The First Few Months

The first few months after your baby is born are crucial. They set the stage for the relationship between your child and your pet. Getting off on a positive note may shorten the time needed for your dog or cat to adjust to the new member of the family and to the animal's new position. A bad first impression is a step backwards and could be a clue to problems lurking ahead. This chapter gives you some ideas of how you can control this adjustment period and how you can lay the foundation of a loving friendship.

Coming Home

After your baby is born, you can start the adjustment period for your dog or cat before the infant comes home. This is accomplished by using your pet's highly developed sense of smell. Have someone bring home a blanket or piece of clothing that has come in contact with the baby; the garment will have the baby's scent on it. Allow your pet to sniff and familiarize itself with the scent. This should be a pleasant experience for your animal; it should be praised and given treats while it explores. This will help your pet make a connection between your baby's scent and good things.

When the mother arrives home, she should greet the pet alone. This is strongly recommended if the mother's stay in the hospital has been long or if she is the person to whom the pet has the strongest attachment. The father should take charge of the baby and not allow the animal to come in contact with him or her.

There are two important reasons for this. First, your pet may be excited and energetic when it sees the mother after an absence. In its frenzy, it might accidentally injure the baby. Second, giving the animal time alone with the mother will show your dog or cat that its relationship with her has not changed and is secure. The bond between the mother and the animal should be re-established before introducing the new baby.

As visitors come to see the new baby, they should also give attention to the animal. Visitors who generally lavish attention on the pet should continue this practice. This will make your pet feel secure; it can also help maintain its routine. In addition, continued attention from visitors will solidify the notion that the new baby can bring positive events.

Introducing Your Pet To Your Child

When the excitement of the mother's return home has died down, it is time to bring your pet and your baby together. Ideally, the introduction should take place away from your pet's territory; if possible, you should introduce them outside the home. A neutral site will keep your dog or cat from asserting its territorial rights. This will reduce the chance of the animal reacting to the new child in an aggressive manner.

It is best to have two people perform the introduction. You can hold the baby while the other person controls the animal. The dog should be commanded to sit and stay. The person controlling the dog should hold the dog by the leash or the collar. If your pet has a tendency to become excited, you might consider placing a muzzle on it. However, if your dog is not accustomed to wearing such a device, the muzzle may make the dog anxious and should probably be avoided.

You should stand, holding the baby, about 10 to 15 feet away from your pet. At this distance, your dog will be able to pick up your child's scent. Gradually carry your infant towards the dog. You should pause every few steps to gauge your pet's reaction. As you approach the animal, both the person holding the dog and you should praise it. If the animal is calm, you may feel comfortable bringing the two together right away. However, if the dog appears agitated or excited as you carry the baby towards it, you may want to conduct the introduction over a period of days. Each day, you can decrease the distance between the two.

The introduction usually takes only a few moments, but the amount of time needed will depend on your dog. When it remains calm as you approach and you feel comfortable, you may allow your dog to sniff the child at a close distance. While you protect the baby's face with your arms, your pet can give your child a close inspection. This sniffing will go a long way to acclimating the dog to the newest member of the family.

You can use the same technique to introduce your baby to a cat. The only variation is that the second person should hold the cat in his or her arms. The introduction should last as long as the cat wishes. As soon as it tries to leave, you should allow it to do so.

Bear in mind that the animal will be able to sense your mood; it will respond to how you react. You should make the introduction in a calm, easy manner. If you are scared or nervous, your pet may sense that something is wrong. It may become excited and anxious. If you remain calm and constantly praise your pet for good behavior, you will increase the chance that the introduction will go smoothly.

After the introduction, your pet may appear to have accepted your baby. However, you must not relax your vigilance. You should never leave your pet unattended when it is around the baby. When you are unable to supervise them, you should take steps to keep the two apart.

Potential Behavioral Problems

During the first 6 to 8 weeks, your pet will learn to accept the infant as part of the family and adjust to the changes brought by the child's arrival. Most pets adjust without problems. After their initial curiousity has been satisfied, they simply accept the new baby as an interesting addition to the family. Some pets, however, do not adjust well.

You need to be especially cautious with a hunting dog or any dog that has exhibited predatory behavior in the past. The noises and movements of a young baby can be confused with those of a prey animal and can elicit instinctive attack responses. But as the child grows, the hunting dog will soon realize that the baby is a person and accept him or her as a family member. This process will be aided by the fact that the child is accepted and loved by the adults in the household. If your dog is poorly socialized and unaccustomed to other people, this adjustment may take several weeks. Until such time that you are totally convinced the animal does not consider your infant as prey, keep the dog on a leash and do not allow it to be near your baby.

Other potential problems stem from a dog's pack behavior. Even if your dog accepts your new baby as part of the family, it may try to establish dominance over the infant. In a dog's social environment, smaller animals and juveniles are usually subservient or prey. Since infants are smaller than most dogs, your pet may act in a domineering fashion.

In addition, an adult canine will discipline annoying pups by growling, nipping or biting. Your dog may view your child in the same fashion as a pup in a pack. This can lead to natural aggression that is more an act of disciplining than of anger.

While these behaviors will probably diminish when your child grows to be bigger than your dog, you must be able to suppress them now. Sternly correcting your pet whenever it displays an aggressive tendency can teach the dog that any aggression is not tolerated. In addition, a dog should never be left alone with a baby.

Sibling rivalry can also be a problem. The attention required by your baby may make your pet appear to be jealous. While it may not be jealous of the baby, the pet can be upset because of the necessary schedule changes. The large block of time given to a new-born child often takes away from the normal attention given to the dog. In a simple sense, the anxious pet may come to view the child as a rival.

To combat this, many people shower the pet with attention and affection when the baby is napping or otherwise out of the way. This usually does not work. Your pet may decide that it is better off when the baby is gone; that will not help the two become friends.

The best way to handle sibling rivalry is by utilizing a concept known as synchronized attention. This is giving your pet lavish attention when the baby is present. You may even want to diminish the amount of attention that you pay your pet when the baby is not around. You may give your pet treats when your child is present and withhold them at other times. If your pet likes to be groomed, you should do that with your baby in the room. Your dog should begin to associate good feelings and affection with the presence of your child.

You can take additional steps as well. Try to include your dog and your baby in each other's activities. For instance, you may allow the dog to watch you change your infant's diapers or give him or her a bath. You may also take the baby with you when you walk the dog. The baby can ride either in a pack or in a stroller.

You should avoid carrying the baby in your arms while holding your dog on a leash. If the dog becomes unruly, you may accidentally drop your child. By the same token, you should never tie the leash to the stroller. If your pet takes off after another animal or a car, it may drag the stroller with it. You should hold the leash in one hand and the stroller with the other. You can use the hand holding the leash for leverage to help push and guide the stroller, but the leash should never be attached to the carriage. A dog that has been trained to heel properly will be able to walk along side the stroller and to follow voice commands as needed.

A behavioral problem that may develop in your cat is that it becomes an "attack cat" and starts to scratch people and furniture. One type of attack cat is suffering from boredom. This boredom stems from receiving less attention following the baby's arrival. To create excitement and release energy, a cat may behave in an aggressive manner such as "attacking" the newspaper as you read it or lunging at your ankles as you walk by. Their activity level and "attacks" probably will increase at night because cats are nocturnal creatures.

You should take steps to alleviate your cat's boredom and lessen the attacks by creating alternative outlets for your cat's energy. If the cat is confined, increase the amount of space in which it can roam. You may want to frequently let the cat out for exercise. In addition, you should provide access to a window where it can view activity and keep itself occupied. When the cat "attacks," you should redirect its attention to a toy. Ping-pong balls, crumpled paper and balls of twine are fun to chase. Catnip toys are also good diversions.

You can also give your cat more attention. Spending a few extra minutes playing with your cat each day may be enough to satisfy the animal. Other creative solutions may also work. Usually, as soon as your cat is no longer bored, its "attack" behavior will cease.

However, an attack cat can be more than bored; it may be unhappy with your infant's arrival. This occasionally happens to a cat that has been the center of attention for many years but is now feeling replaced by the baby. The increased activity associated with the new arrival will upset the cat's normal routine. The animal may act as though it is angry, frustrated or jealous. While the child is the indirect root of the behavior, the animal focuses its displeasure by attacking people or urinating on household objects.

Unlike a bored cat, this animal will not respond to your attempts to eliminate its aggressive actions with diversions. Instead, you can try to alleviate this situation by using the synchronized attention approach already discussed. Once your cat associates increased attention from you with the presence of the baby, it may alter its negative behavior. You can also try the water pistol method to stop unwarranted behavior.

The positive approach of synchronized attention coupled with the negative effects of the water pistol method should stop your cat's attack behavior. If this behavior does not subside, however, your cat will be a risk to your baby. If the cat tries to attack the baby or it continues its aggression towards other people and objects, you should seek professional help.

One last point needs to be made about potential behavior problems. Dogs and cats have extremely sensitive ears. The plaintive crying of newborn infant can be very irritating or stressful for an animal. If your pet acts upset, it should be able to get away from the ruckus. Allow your dog or cat to go outside or find a quiet corner of the house.

There is no way to predict how long it will take before your pet becomes accustomed to your baby. Some animals will adjust within a couple of days; others may gradually accept the child over the course of several weeks. If your pet has not adjusted after a period of 4-8 weeks, you should consult your veterinarian or trainer. A professional may be able to help you determine whether the problem can be overcome or is insurmountable. In either case, your veterinarian or trainer should be able to recommend steps to take that will remedy the situation.

However, if at any time during the adjustment period, your dog or cat demonstrates any aggressive behavior directly towards your child, contact a pet professional immediately. Your child's safety may depend on your rapid response.

Babysitters

At some time, almost every family will have an outsider involved with a baby's care. Some households only need a babysitter for an occasional evening out; others need full-time help. Whether the sitter is there for one hour or forty, it is important that everyone involved, including the pet, be comfortable with the arrangements. This will ensure the maintenance of your child's security.

Ideally, your babysitter will like animals. She should be willing to give your pet some attention during her work hours. In this manner, she can develop a positive relationship with the animal. At a minimum, however, she must not be afraid of your pet. A sitter that is fearful of animals may evoke an aggressive response or be unable to discipline your pet if necessary. In that case, she may not be able to maintain control of your household while you are gone and cannot guarantee the safety of your child.

You can help your sitter by introducing her to the dog or cat before she starts working. If you have a dog, you should also teach her your pet's obedience commands and have her demonstrate her ability to use them properly. This way, she will be able to communicate with your dog in the same way that you do.

Once you are certain that the sitter can control your pet, you need to give her detailed instructions regarding the household routines. Explain all the steps that are taken to ensure the baby's safety, including supervised pet visits and separate sleeping arrangements. Show her where the pet is allowed and what areas are off-limits. Your instructions for the animal should be just as detailed as they are for the baby. This will ensure that the interactions between your pet and child are handled exactly as you would like them to be.

Although rare, there is another problem that can develop. If your dog is very protective of your child, it may view the babysitter as a threat to the baby. The animal may prevent your sitter from approaching and caring for the youngster. You can help prevent this by acclimating the pet to the sitter's role as a care-giver. This should be done after the dog and she have become well-acquainted. Then have the sitter hold the baby while you are present to reassure the dog. After a few exposures, the dog should be adjusted to the sitter and you should be able to leave them without worry.

Adjusting to a new babysitter takes time. So does adapting to all of the lifestyle changes that accompany a new baby. By the end of the first few months, however, your pet should be comfortable with the new schedule and the unusual sights, sounds and smells of the new arrival. And even if your child and your pet are not best friends yet, a solid foundation will have been laid for a relationship of love and trust.

Chapter Eight
Growing Together

As your baby grows, his or her relationship with your pet will change. Each stage of a child's development will bring new opportunities to forge and solidify a strong friendship with a dog or cat. However, each stage will also present new challenges to overcome and potential problems to avoid.

Your Pet's Perspective

Each stage that your child goes through (infant, toddler, preschooler and beyond) will cause your child to be viewed differently by your pet. Your pet may not understand that the active three year old is the same child as the crying infant whose nursery it could not enter. To your dog or cat, your child will be a new creature at each stage of his or her life. Most animals, dogs in particular, will react more to the behaviors undertaken by a child than the child itself.

The result is that your pet will need to be acclimated to your youngster at every stage of development. You cannot be confident that your dog or cat, having accepted your child as a baby, will accept him or her as a toddler. Close supervision of the interactions between your pet and your child should enable you to determine if your animal is having trouble adjusting.

From Baby To Toddler

Problems between children and pets often do not arise until the children become mobile. When children are very young and are unable to crawl, they cannot actively annoy or challenge a pet. They may even be looked upon by a dog or a cat as a good food source, as evident from the tidbits of food dropped or thrown from highchairs.

Most children will find a dog or a cat to be a constant source of wonder. As soon as your baby can crawl, he or she will probably want to investigate and to play with the furry, four-legged member of the family. Your dog or cat, however, may interpret this new attention as an annoyance or possibly even as aggression.

You must closely supervise the interaction between your child and pet. Even if your pet has been good-natured and accepted your baby right from the start, it may now perceive your child to be a threat. A cat would probably rather be alone and simply run away from an inquisitive baby. For this reason, a cat probably will not be a threat to a toddler unless the animal is cornered and cannot escape.

A good rule is to have at least one safe retreat for your cat in each room of your house. A safe retreat is a place where the cat can rest or sleep without being disturbed by your child. In the kitchen, you might clear off the top of the refrigerator or a cabinet. A cat door to the basement or outside will work; it is generally too small for a child to crawl through. Blocking off a doorway with a gate can also serve as an escape device; most cats can jump over a gate and leave the child behind. In a family room, a bookshelf beyond the reach of a child would work well.

On the other hand, a dog is a different matter. You should take some steps to prevent a problem from developing. If you have not used a crate as a den for your dog, consider doing so now. As previously discussed, a crate will help protect both your dog and your child. The dog may use the crate as a haven from unwanted attention and you can confine the dog in the crate when you are unable to closely supervise your pet and child. An airline-type crate, with its solid plastic sides, prohibits a child from sticking his or her fingers or any other objects into the crate. An open crate that has been covered with a blanket accomplishes the same thing. However, most crates have wire mesh openings that, while providing air and visibility for the dog, also give inquisitive fingers access to the pet. For this reason, you should not leave your child alone with your dog, even if your pet is secured in its crate.

Your child should be instructed never to crawl into the crate and not to bother the dog when it is resting there. Consistency is important with your child as well as with your pets; you must always firmly tell your child "no" when he or she attempts to disturb the dog in the crate.

As your child's mobility increases, you will have to decide what to do about your pet door. Such doors are designed to give your dog or cat ready access to the outside. However, they can do the same for your toddler. Your child could fall down a flight of stairs or escape to the yard if the pet door is not secure. One solution is to keep the pet door fastened whenever the child is in the area. If that is not feasible, shut the pet door permanently or replace the entire door with one that does not have an opening for animals. This will necessitate letting your pet out every so often but it will keep your child inside.

Another possible solution is to replace the pet door with a new pet door that opens electronically. A door such as this is locked at all times. It comes with a device that fits on your pet's collar. As the animal approaches the door, the device will trigger a mechanism that opens the door automatically. (Of course, this device will not prevent your child from leaving when the pet does!)

Toys are a potential source of danger for both children and pets. Small parts that rip or break off can be swallowed by a child or an animal. Make sure that the toys that you purchase are safe for both your child and your pet.

Do not allow your pet and child to play with each other's toys. Dogs in particular may be possessive and react aggressively if a child plays with its toys. Your child should be instructed not to play with bones or toys that the dog may have buried in the yard. At the same time, you should consistently correct your dog if it plays with any of your child's toys. When the toys are not being used, you should keep your child's toys separate from those of your pet; a toy box for each will accomplish this.

Also, it is a good idea to limit the number of toys for your pet. This way, your pet learns exactly what belongs to it and that it should leave all other toys alone. Two or three toys are sufficient. You might give a dog a rawhide bone and a nylon chew. A cat might like a catnip mouse and a ping-pong ball.

If you want your child to have a sandbox in the yard, you should consider buying or building one that can be covered. A cover will deny your pet access to the box. This will prevent a cat from using it as a litter box or a dog from burying bones there. Sandboxes that come with a cover are available in a variety of shapes and sizes.

Another important step is to place your animal's food and water bowl in a spot where your child cannot get to them. A cat's food dish can be put on a counter or table that your child cannot reach. A child gate can also be used to separate the bowls from an inquisitive toddler. A non-spill water dish will prevent your baby from tipping over your pet's water.

If you feed your pet using the "free choice" method, you may want to change your policy. Free choice feeding means that food is always available for your pet. A better plan is to feed your dog or cat at specific times during the day and to monitor your child while the animal is eating. This will prevent your child from playing in your pet's food; it also diminishes the chance of an aggressive response from an animal that thinks your child is stealing its food.

The Best Protection: Increased Vigilance

The most important way to prevent problems is to increase your supervision of your child as he or she begins to explore. Your crawler will be beginning to understand the meaning of the word "no" but cannot be expected to respond in a reliable fashion for many months. You will have to constantly steer your baby away from danger.

Most incidents between pets and children arise when a child tries to take the animal's food or awakes it from a sound sleep. Disturbing an animal that is eating or sleeping can be dangerous; you should not let your child wander too close to your pet unless your dog or cat appears to be ready for the attention.

Even when your pet accepts your child's attention, you should be on guard. A very young child lacks sufficient motor control to always be gentle; he or she may unintentionally hit and hurt the dog or cat. Many children like to hug your pet or pull its hair and tail. You should instruct your child not to perform these actions but you cannot expect a baby or toddler to understand or obey consistently. Remove your baby immediately if you notice that he or she is starting to annoy your pet. You probably do not have to worry about your cat being provoked. A feline will usually escape a child's clutches before the situation becomes a crisis.

However, a dog, being a social animal, may allow the child to annoy it beyond its point of tolerance. If your dog responds as it normally would to a bothersome puppy, the animal may growl and nip at your child. Your pet must learn that this is not acceptable.

You may be able to desensitize your dog to aggressive behavior by your child. To attempt this, you need to closely monitor the interactions between your dog and child. You should praise and reward your dog when it is accepting of the child's actions and sternly reprimand it if it shows any signs of aggression. You should also separate the two so that the child cannot excessively annoy the animal or be hurt. Over time, the dog may begin to accept hugs, hair and tail pulls and other actions by your child as normal aspects of life.

You should consult with your veterinarian, dog trainer or behavioral specialist, however, before trying any behavioral modification training. Teaching your dog to overcome an instinctive response is a difficult task but it can be accomplished with consistent, positive reinforcement.

Training Exercises That Involve Your Toddler

At this stage, you can begin to train the animal to respect and obey your child. Desentizing your dog to the minor irritations caused by an inquisitive baby or toddler is one way to teach your pet to be tolerant of your child. Another method is to include your child in the general care of the dog. For instance, your child should be present when you feed the dog or bathe it. Explain what you are doing, even if the baby is too young to comprehend. Eventually, your child will start to understand some of the basic aspects of caring for your pet. Within a short period of time, your child may begin to participate. A toddler can bring you the food bowl for filling and can help soap a dog in the bath.

It is a good idea to include your baby in your dog's training exercises. You can put your pet through its paces while your baby is in a backpack. You can also take your child with you when you walk the dog. This will be instructive and pleasant for both your child and your pet.

As your toddler begins to speak and control his or her motions, you can have your child try some commands. For instance, your child may be able to properly use the "sit" or "down" commands. When your dog obeys, you should lavishly praise it. It is imperative, however, that you still hold the leash while your child is giving commands; you must maintain control of the situation at all times.

Preschooler and Beyond

As your child enters the preschool years, you may wish to involve him or her in the care of your pet. By giving a child some responsibility for the family pet, you will accomplish several things. First, putting your child in the position of care-giver may help to solidify the child's role as a dominant member of the family. Second, even minor responsibility for the well-being of another living thing will help teach your child to be sensitive to the needs of others. A third benefit will be the creation of positive interactions between your child and pet.

This responsibility, however, should not be taken lightly and you should be careful not to overload your child before he or she is ready for the tasks. Each child is an individual; you must be the judge of how much your child can handle and when additional jobs can be assigned. A child can feel overwhelmed by too much responsibility at a young age. And if you do not closely supervise and follow up on the quality of care, your pet may suffer.

At the preschooler age, a child cannot adequately care for an animal alone. However, he or she may be able to assist you in various tasks. For instance, a preschooler can help you feed your pet. This assistance can be as simple as calling the pet when it is time to eat or as holding the dish still on the counter or table while you place the food in it. As the child matures, you can increase his or her role.

Another area where a preschooler can help is grooming. A young child can help you soap a dog when giving your pet a bath. If your child can be gentle and your dog is calm, your child may be able to brush the animal. You should closely supervise so that order is maintained.

As your child matures, you can begin to assign more responsibilty. At some point, you may be able to have your child walk the dog without supervision. Three criteria must be met before allowing the child and the dog to go out alone. First, the walker must be physically large enough to handle the animal. If you have a Doberman Pinscher or Labrador Retriever, your dog may be too big and strong to be controlled by your child. If your dog consistently pulls your child along when walking, you should not let your child handle the leash alone until he or she is older.

Second, you must be confident that your child can walk your dog in the correct manner and that he or she will know how to react in any given situation. Instruct your child to hold the end of the leash firmly in one hand and not to wrap the leash around the wrist or tie it to clothing. The other hand should hold the leash at a comfortable level and be used to guide the dog.

Third, the dog must be extremely well trained. It must respond quickly and correctly to your child's commands. If it does not, you may have a situation where you can trust your child but not your dog. Without total confidence in both, they should not be allowed to go for a walk without adult supervision.

If you have an older child and are expecting a new baby, now may the the perfect time to allow the older child to assume more of the responsibility for the animal's care. Explain to your child that your dog or cat will need more attention and affection than usual once the new baby arrives. You can then enlist your older child's help.

Preschool children tend to interact with animals in a variety of ways. Many affectionate intentions of a child towards a dog or cat are interpreted by the animal as aggressive advances. The animal, especially a dog, may react by growling or otherwise showing that it is annoyed. One potential danger is that your child may misinterpret your dog's bared teeth to be a smile. As a result, your child may continue his or her behavior without realizing that the animal is ready to bite.

Some children purposely put themselves in danger. While a child may want to interact with a pet, the animal may ignore the youngster unless disturbed by him or her. To get the animal's attention, the youth may annoy the dog or cat. The child does not want to be hurt; he or she just wants to be noticed. Since the annoying behavior does elicit a response (albeit a negative one), the youngster may continue to pester the animal. The child may end up being injured if his or her behavior is not corrected.

In addition, some children will redirect anger or frustration toward the family pet. The old saying about kicking a dog at the end of a hard day applies to children as well as adults. You should be particularly alert to the interactions between your pet and your child when he or she is upset. Swift action to stop mistreatment of your pet may prevent the animal from unleashing an aggressive reaction.

The Death of a Pet

Some parents wonder what to tell their children when a beloved pet dies or must be euthanized. Although the decision how to handle this situation is a personal one for every family, it is often best to tell the child the truth about what has happened to your dog or cat. Many children have their first experience with death when a family pet dies. While this is a difficult period, it does provide an opportunity for a child to begin to understand that death is a part of life. Children may learn about your feelings and their own while you grieve together about the loss.

If possible, conduct a burial service. Many

children learn from participating in the burial; some may want to have a memorial service for your pet. (Before burying any animal in your backyard, check with your local health department to see if such an act is allowed.)

Many parents are tempted to console their children after the death of a pet by getting a new one. It may be better to wait a while before replacing a pet. Children, like adults, need time to deal with their grief and sadness. It may be several weeks, months or even longer before the family has fully accepted the loss of a pet and is ready for a new best friend.

Chapter Nine
Educating Your Child About Your Pet

You should begin to teach your child at a very young age how to interact with your pet and other animals. "Formal" education cannot begin until your child has developed to the point of being able to retain and follow your instructions. But from the earliest days, your child will mimic your actions. If you treat your pet properly, your child will probably learn to do so as well. Correcting and disciplining improper behavior will reinforce the lessons.

The Need For Education

Early education is critical. A child that knows how to act around animals will be able to enjoy a pet and develop a healthy bond with it. On the other hand, a child who does not know how to behave may inadvertently provoke an aggressive response from the animal. Very young children may not learn from their mistakes; they may not make the connection that pulling the hair of a dog leads to the dog taking a nip at them. Older children may learn the lesson but for the wrong reason. Rather than learning to respect the rights of your pet, they simply become afraid of all animals. This can prevent a child from developing a positive relationship with any animal. It could also lead to bigger problems, since a dog may sense that such a child can be dominated.

A preschooler should know the basics of how to act around an animal. The reason for this is that the risk of dog and cat bites tends to increase somewhat when a child is 4 to 5 years old. At this age, children tend to spend more time outdoors than when they were toddlers and may have access to other animals in the neighborhood. Their playing, running, screaming and general mayhem can excite an animal, especially one that does not know the children well. A preschooler who is able to recognize the signs of annoyance and aggression in an animal may be able to avoid any unfortunate incident.

Your child should be taught not to tease an animal. This includes poking a pet in order to get a reaction. Teasing can make a dog or cat mean and intolerant of all advances by your child. This may result in an aggressive response that could lead to an injury, either during the teasing episode or any time that your child approaches your pet.

One of the best methods for teaching a young child how to act around a pet utilizes a stuffed animal. With a stuffed dog or cat, you can show your child how to approach, hold, pet and play with an animal. The youngster can then practice on the toy. This enables your child to learn how to behave without scaring or annoying your dog or cat. It also allows the child to make mistakes without suffering the consequences of an adverse reaction from a live animal.

Even after your child has learned how to act and react around an animal, you must keep monitoring your child's interaction with your pet. Most children need constant reinforcement of rules to avoid lapses. Regarding safety, there is no substitute for adult supervision.

When To Approach an Animal

The first lesson that should be taught is when to approach an animal. The only time that your child should consider petting a dog or cat is when an adult who is clearly in control of the animal invites your child to meet it.

There are some general rules to teach your child about when not to approach an animal. A basic premise is that a dog or a cat should not be disturbed when it is eating. An animal, by nature, will protect its food. Your pet may interpret a disturbance as an attempt to take its food away and may react forcefully. While your dog or cat should be taught to accept this action, your child should be taught to avoid it. Until your child understands that he or she should not bother the pet while it is eating, you may find it necessary to remove him or her from the room. You should also have separate eating areas for your pet and your child.

The youth should also learn not to approach your pet when it is sleeping. An animal that is awakened suddenly will be startled and may snap or bite. By the same token, your child should learn not to sneak up on a pet, even if it is awake. Teach your child to call out your pet's name as he or she approaches it. Hearing its name will alert the animal that your child is approaching.

Of course, both your child and you should be especially sensitive to the needs of pets that are old or infirm. A lively toddler should not be allowed to annoy a venerable old dog or cat, even if the animal is good-natured. As your pet ages, it may become less tolerant of children. Subjecting it to the exploits of a rambunctious child can be unpleasant for the pet and may incite an aggressive response.

A child should never approach any animal that

is sick or injured. When in pain, even the most gentle pet may resist any effort to touch it and may struggle or bite. Instruct your child to come get you or another adult if your pet is injured; under no circumstances should he or she attempt to aid the animal. (If your pet is injured, you should use extreme caution; as already stated, an animal in pain is dangerous. Contact your veterinarian immediately to obtain instructions on what to do.)

Teach your child to never approach any strange animal. Even a dog or cat that appears to be friendly can be dangerous. It is possible that the animal is afraid of your child and may bite. Fearful animals will usually attempt to run away; instruct your child not to chase a fleeing animal.

Even a dog on a leash should be not be approached without an adult's consent. A leash can easily be caught or wrapped around a child's arms, legs or neck. Serious injury can result if this were to happen and the animal became excited.

Your child should never enter a house or yard to visit an animal unless the owner offers an invitation. Animals can be very territorial. A dog or cat that may have reacted in a friendly manner towards your child outside of the animal's yard may be aggressive when your child enters the animal's territory. This is especially true of dogs that are tied up in the yard. For the same reason, your child should be instructed never to reach through a fence or car window to pet a dog or a cat.

Before approaching an animal, your child should make sure that it is in a friendly, relaxed mood. Aggressive or fearful animals should be avoided. A youngster can learn to understand an animal by watching its body language and behavior. Even though pets do not talk, they constantly communicate with people and other animals.

In general, a dog that is friendly and submissive will act like a puppy or young dog. A dog in a friendly mood and eager to play will display certain signs. Some of these are listed below:

- Tail is wagging or down
- Ears are relaxed and moving to catch sounds
- Rolling on its side or on its back
- Crouching down with its hindquarters raised and its head on the front paws (also known as play bowing)

A cat that is friendly and receptive will have a relaxed looking body and calm facial expression. If the cat is lying down, it may continue to do so or even roll over on its back. If the cat is standing, it may approach and rub against the visitor. Look for the following signs from a relaxed cat:

- Ears pointed forward and outward
- Ears moving freely to catch sounds
- Purring
- Tail stretched out or held erect

- Head tilted to one side
- Short, repeated meows

Your child must understand, however, that not every friendly dog and cat wants to be petted or played with. Advise your child to get permission from an adult before approaching the animal.

How To Approach and Play With an Animal

If a supervising adult invites your child to meet a dog, he or she may approach the animal in a quiet, nonaggressive manner. Your child should offer an outstretched hand for the dog to sniff; the fingers should be curled inward. The dog may sniff other parts of the body to get further acquainted. Once the dog has accepted the offered hand, your child will probably be able to gently pet the animal under the chin or on the chest.

When petting and playing with a dog, your child should learn not to act in a manner that can be interpreted as threatening by the dog. Such an interpretation may spark an aggressive response by the animal. Your child should not pat the dog on top of the head or make any fast, jerky motions. Instruct your child not to stare into the eyes of a dog. In addition, you should closely supervise their interaction if your child is running, yelling or roughhousing with or near your dog. This behavior may elicit a "chase" response from the animal. Your child should be aware that many dogs use their mouths and teeth to play in a rough manner; your child runs the risk of being bitten if he or she persists in roughhousing with your dog.

A youngster should also be careful about playing with a dog's possessions. Even though it is not acceptable behavior, a dog may be overly protective of its food, treats and toys. A female dog who has just had puppies may bite anyone who approaches her offspring without her consent. Your child must learn to respect your dog's things, especially if those things are cute little puppies.

When greeting a cat, a youth should walk quietly towards the animal. Running, yelling and grabbing the cat are not permitted. The child may want to squat or bend down, then offer the cat an outstretched hand. If the cat accepts this action, he or she can then gently stroke the animal behind the ears and under the chin.

Children should be cautioned not to pet the cat's body or belly. Unlike dogs, cats do not want their abdomen rubbed. Many felines feel threatened when their bellies are touched and react by biting or scratching.

Because cats can change their minds quickly, children should also learn to understand a cat's signals after the initial introduction. A cat that is enjoying the attention will remain relaxed, purr, partially close its eyes and tilt its ears outward. If the child is kneeling or standing, the cat may rub against the child's legs and make small hopping motions on its hind feet. Contented cats sitting on a youngster's lap may attempt to "knead" the child's legs or clothing with their front paws.

In contrast, a frightened or angry cat may hiss, spit or growl. The cat may use its front paw to take a swipe at the child or attempt to grab the youngster's arm. A cat that is starting to get irritated may lightly nip the person petting it. If the cat appears at all anxious or upset, the child should cease petting it and leave the cat alone.

Signs of Aggression or Fear In an Animal

Even more critical than knowing when a dog is friendly is recognizing when a dog is showing aggression or fear. Knowing when to avoid a dog may be the most important lesson that you can teach your child. This knowledge will reduce the chance of encountering a dangerous predicament.

A dog that is aggressive will try to make itself appear larger; this is accomplished by raising its hackles (the hair on the back and the neck). The other common signs of aggression displayed by a dog are listed below. Neither your child nor you should venture near a dog that is showing one or a combination of them.

- Hackles (the fur on its back and the neck) are up
- Ears erect and pointing forward
- Tail up and stiff
- Staring into the eyes
- Growling or snarling
- Baring its teeth
- Standing, leaning forward with its legs rigid.

The signs of fear are essentially the same. The only difference is that the physical exhibition by the dog may be somewhat understated. And it may show signs of fear and aggression at the same time. For instance, the hackles may be up and the ears may be erect but the dog might be cowering slightly. Another example is that the tail may be down or wagging but the dog might be growling or backing away. A frightened animal can easily become an aggressive one. Your child should learn to avoid these dogs as well.

Cats, while more likely to run away if annoyed than dogs, can be aggressive and pose a threat to children. Your child should know the signs of aggression in these animals, too. One of the key determinants is the ears. A cat that is relaxed will slowly move its ears in several directions to absorb as many different sounds as possible. If the cat should pick up an interesting noise or a sound that indicated imminent danger, the ears will focus on it. An irritated, nervous or frustrated cat will rapidly twitch its ears back and forth. An aggressive cat will rotate its ears so the backs are visible.

In addition, just like dogs, cats will try to make themselves appear larger when they are feeling aggressive or threatened. Thus, even a small kitten will arch its back and make its hair erect, much like a drawing of a "Halloween cat." The other common signs of a cat that feels threatened are listed below.

- Back arched
- Hair on back and neck raised
- Pupils dilated
- Hissing, growling, whining or spitting sounds
- Stiff, stretched legs
- Tail twitching or dropped with hair raised
- Ears rotated back and flattened against head

Make sure that that your child knows to avoid a cat that is exhibiting any of these signs. As with dogs, your child should not ever intervene in a cat fight. If your cat has been in a fight, neither your child nor you should approach it immediately afterwards. If the cat is still in an aggressive mood, it may redirect its anger to whoever approaches. It is better to wait until the cat has taken on another activity, such as playing or grooming, before handling it.

Encountering an Aggressive Animal

As mentioned earlier, the single most important lesson that you can teach your child is to
recognize the signs that a dog is being aggressive
and to avoid that animal. However, your child must
also know what to do if an aggressive dog cannot be
avoided.

There are steps that you should teach your child
to take in the unlikely event that he or she is threatened by a dog. They are listed below.

- Do not run. Sudden movement may incite
  the dog.
- Do not yell or scream. Loud noises may
  also encourage the dog.
- Do not stare into the animal's eyes.
- Stand still, if the dog approaches to sniff.
  Most dogs will go away once they know
  that a child is not a threat.
- Back away slowly and calmly, if the dog's
  attention is diverted or it begins to leave.
- Watch where the dog goes, if it leaves.
- Walk away in the opposite direction. Do
  not run.

In the event of a dog attack, your child should
know that the best action is to curl up in a ball or lie
flat on the stomach. In either case, your child should
try to protect the face. With luck, the animal may

stop and go away without inflicting a serious injury. Fortunately, the chances of grave injuries resulting from a vicious attack are very remote.

Cats usually avoid trouble. They run away from inquisitive children. Because of this behavior trait and their small size, aggressive cats are rarely a problem. They do not usually make unsolicited attacks on children. Teach your child to avoid a frightened or hostile cat by walking away.

What To Do If Bitten By an Animal

You should explain to your child what to do if a dog, cat or any other animal bites them. The most critical aspect is to have the child let you know that he or she has been bitten. It is important that the child understands that he or she will not be punished for telling you, even if the animal was provoked by the child. If you learn that your child has been bitten, you should take action immediately.

Contact your physician. This should be done in all cases, regardless of how minor the injury appears. Even the smallest wound can be dangerous. Animals carry tiny microbes in their mouths and paws that can lead to infection if the wound is not treated properly. Your physician will most likely advise you to wash the wound with soap and water and to bring your child in for an examination.

Find out what kind of animal bit your child. If it was a wild animal, you will need to take your child to a doctor to determine whether preventive rabies treatment is necessary.

Ask your child about the animal, if a dog or cat did the biting.

- Does your child or any friends know whose pet it was?
- What did it look like?
- Did it have on a collar and a tag?
- Where did it come from and in what direction did it go after the incident?

Contact your local police or public health department. The animal may need to to be quarantined to see if it has any of the symptoms of rabies. If the owner of the animal can be found, you may be able to get a record of recent rabies vaccination. Even if the shots are up to date, the animal may need to be isolated for a short period of time.

Reducing the Risk Of an Attack

There is little reported information on cat bites and attacks. However, there are an estimated one to three million reported dog bites each year; countless more are unreported. Even though the overall number of deaths due to dog bites is relatively low, the greatest percentage of fatalities are children under the age of 10 years old. Children are frequent victims because they are very active outdoors. Their playing and behavior can excite a dog and may be interpreted as threatening actions. This undoubtedly causes some dogs to react aggressively. Children are also likely not to recognize a dog's aggressive or fearful body posture. They may not realize that the animal is likely to bite.

Most bites suffered by children are on the arms and legs. However, many children sustain wounds on their faces. The reason for this is that a child's face is generally close to the level of a dog's mouth. And many children have the tendency of approaching a dog face-to-face.

The newspaper and television tend to hype bites and attacks inflicted by strays or "killer" dogs such as pit bulls. Many bites, however, come from dogs that are around the neighborhood and that, for the most part, are not vicious. These dogs get along with their own families; unfortunately, they cannot tolerate other children. Most neighborhoods would be safer if all of the dogs in it were neutered and well trained. Also, a dog that has been socialized with people and children since being a puppy is less likely to cause a threat.

The chances of a dog bite or attack would diminish significantly if all owners in the neighborhood prevented their dogs from roaming free. A dog that has the run of the neighborhood may establish boundaries for its territory that extend outside the domain of its owner. Once boundaries are set, a dog will protect its territory. A child, inadvertently wandering into a dog's territory, may cause the animal to react to a perceived threat.

Not allowing dogs to roam would reduce the chance of dog fights erupting. Instruct your child not to intervene in a dog fight, even if your own pet is involved and may be injured. Your child should be taught to move away quickly but calmly and to call an adult to the scene. Many children (and adults) are injured when they try to get between the animals. In the frenzy of a dog fight, all people and animals in the immediate vicinity are at risk. If you must attempt to break up a dog fight, spray or throw water on the animals. But take care not to get caught between them.

Chapter Ten
Problems and
What To Do

Most dogs and cats adjust well to a baby. As soon as your pet understands that your infant is part of the family, it will most likely accept the newest member and grow to love him or her.

But you still need to be alert. The time when problems usually begin to occur is when your child becomes mobile. At this point, the interaction between your pet and child will increase significantly. You must learn to recognize the danger signs of a developing problem. If you do, you may be able to prevent a serious incident from occurring.

Signs Of a Developing Problem

Not every animal reacts aggressively the first time that it becomes upset or angry with a child. Many dogs and cats will exhibit evidence of a developing problem before becoming a threat to a child. You should look for any unusual behavior patterns that develop after the arrival of your child. Some changes in your pet's behavior are to be expected; a new addition will dramatically change the lifestyle of everyone in the household. But repeated incidents of misbehaving or unusual activity should be taken as something more serious than a temporary adjustment.

The most common signs of a developing problem displayed by a dog are listed below.

- Excessive barking
- Increased possessiveness of its toys and food
- Excessive chewing or licking of feet and flanks
- Loss of housebreaking skills
- Chewing household objects
- Hiding
- Loss of appetite
- Constantly seeking attention (often by pushing between the child and you)

The most common signs of a developing problem displayed by a cat are listed below.

- Scratching or biting itself
- Increased possessiveness of its toys and food
- Not using the litter box
- Hiding
- Loss of appetite

The key to recognizing one of these signs is to think back on the normal behavior of your pet. If you can remember how the animal normally acted before the baby arrived or became mobile, you should be able to determine if its behavior has changed significantly. Once you have established that your pet is having trouble, you should take steps to help it.

Solving a developing problem begins with understanding the cause of your pet's strange behavior. Some abnormal actions are not directly attributed to the child. Instead, they are caused by related factors such as abrupt changes in routine or decreased amounts of exercise. You may be able to solve these problems by establishing a set routine and giving the animal time to adjust to the new schedule. You should also allow your pet to use up its excess energy by increasing its exercise.

However, the child may be cause of the problem. Dogs and cats covet and protect their relationships with the members of their family. When a new baby arrives, however, the amount of time spent with a pet is often diminished. The attention originally given to the animal now goes to the child. This can cause a negative reaction by your dog or cat. Even though behaviorists believe that your pet will not actually feel jealousy or anger towards your child, the animal can feel threatened, insecure and anxious.

As discussed earlier, a new-born infant or a child that is becoming active may upset a dog's understanding of its place in the hierarchy of the family pack. Your new baby may look small and submissive but the child is treated as a dominant pack member. You should strive to reduce your pet's insecurities and to clarify its relationship within the family pack.

You may be able to do this by involving your child in some of your pet's normal activities and by implementing behavior modification techniques. These were discussed in Chapter Seven and Chapter Eight. These steps will increase the time and attention that you give your pet. They will also help your pet associate good things with your child, recognize the baby as part of the family and understand the hierarchy of the pack. If your pet can reach those goals, you will have eliminated the cause of the problem and the unusual behavior should cease.

It is possible, however, that the root cause of your pet's problem is not related to your child. Many of the listed signs of a developing behavior problem in a dog or cat are exactly the same as those exhibited by a sick animal. For example, if your pet loses its housebreaking skills, it may be frustrated by a new child. On the other hand, it could be suffering from a bladder infection, kidney stones or even a liver problem. Hiding, loss of appetite and chewing on itself can also be signs of illnesses. This is especially true of cats; felines have a tendency to display behavior changes as the only "symptoms" of many illnesses. If your cat stays under the bed after you bring your baby home, it may not be hiding from the new arrival. It may be sick.

If your dog or cat is ill, it will not respond to your efforts to bring the child closer to it. And you may actually set their relationship back. As mentioned in the discussion of health maintenance, an animal that is not feeling well may aggressively overreact to the innocent attentions of a youngster.

Before beginning the exercises to modify your pet's behavior, you should examine the animal for any overt signs of illness and take it to your veterinarian for a check-up. If your pet is sick, identifying and treating the medical problem may solve the behavioral problem. If the animal is not sick, you can then concentrate on behavioral modification. In addition, your veterinarian may have some good advice on how to bring about the desired changes in your pet.

If there is still a problem after establishing that your pet is in good health and trying the various modification techniques, you should consult a pet professional. Animal trainers and behavioral specialists have extensive experience in solving this type of problem. Another advantage of contacting somebody about your case is that the professional will bring in an objective viewpoint. If there is a conflict brewing between a beloved pet and a child that you adore, you may be too emotionally caught up in their plight to formulate an adequate solution.

A third party whose emotions are not involved may be in a better position to diagnose and solve the problem.

No matter how you address your particular situation, the important thing is to get it resolved. One that continues to develop can escalate into a predicament where your child could be in physical danger. You must take action before that happens.

Signs of Imminent Danger For Your Child

In extreme cases, you may notice blatant signs of aggression in your pet. These signs are quite obvious. Even those unfamiliar with animal behavior can usually tell when a dog or cat is ready to strike. If you see one or more of these signs, you must assume that your child is in danger and you must take immediate action to ensure his or her protection.

The most common signs of a dog being an immediate threat are listed below.

- Growling
- Hair raised on back
- Snapping
- Snarling
- Baring its teeth
- Body posture very rigid with weight forward

The most common signs of a cat being an

immediate threat are listed below.

- Growling
- Hissing
- Raised hair on back
- Scratching and clawing
- Biting

Fortunately, most animals will not strike without warning. Some will use different signs to display degrees of annoyance or anger. Canines may vocalize (by grumbling or growling) before physically attacking. The growl usually becomes more pronounced or heavier as the dog becomes angrier and more likely to lash out. The same is true of cats that are hissing. You should try to learn your pet's unique vocabulary. Then, when confronted with a situation, you may be able to determine when the animal is slightly annoyed and when it is dangerously aggressive. However, you must understand that any growling or hissing is a serious sign of aggression and should be treated accordingly.

Heavy growling or hissing, snarling or baring teeth does indicate a grave problem. An animal displaying any of these signs is prepared to attack. A dog or cat such as this should not be allowed near your child, even if the two of them are closely supervised. The potential danger is too great.

However, you should be aware that your pet may not always give advance notice of an aggressive response. If sufficiently provoked or annoyed, even the most placid and good-natured animal can strike without warning. You must be on guard whenever your child interacts with your dog or cat.

What To Do If Your Pet Threatens Your Child

The first step to take if your child is the target of an aggressive action by an animal is to protect the youngster. This is best accomplished by separating your child and your pet. You should either remove the child or the animal from the immediate area. Putting a sufficient distance between the two will ensure that your pet will not be able to harm the child.

The next step is to severely punish the animal for its behavior. It is important, however, that you use a form of punishment that the animal understands. For instance, a dog that has been obedience trained will probably understand the meaning of the terms "no" and "bad dog." A sternly emphatic vocalization of those will let the dog know it has behaved in an unacceptable manner. On the other hand, the dog may not understand a physical correction. If you have never hit your dog, it probably will not make the connection that the blow was a result of its behavior. It will only become scared of you. A physical correction such as vigorously shaking the animal can be effective but only if the animal understands the method of correction before the incident occurs.

Another issue concerning punishment involves timing. You must punish your pet within such a time frame that it remembers why it is being reprimanded. For instance, your dog snapped at your child. This action scared the toddler and caused the child to cry. In an effort to protect and comfort the child, you pick him up, rush to another room where the dog cannot get in and hold the child until he stops crying. After that, you go back and sternly punish the dog. The problem is that, by the time you get back to the animal, it does not remember that snapping at the child is the reason for the punishment. A better scenario would be to make sure that the child is safe, quickly correct the animal and then go comfort the child.

One last point regarding punishment needs to be made. You cannot assume that proper correction will prevent an aggressive response from happening again. Just because your pet understands that its behavior was unacceptable this time does not mean that it will act properly in the future. The situation is too risky to be left to chance. You have to be certain that your pet will not pose another threat to your child.

One step to take to help prevent a recurrence of the aggression is to evaluate the events that immediately preceded the incident. It is possible that the aggressive act by your pet was the direct result of some action taken by your child. For instance, your youngster may like to climb on the pet or to pull on its ears and tail. While your child did not mean any harm, his or her action may have been perceived as a threat and may have even hurt the animal. The dog or cat then responded accordingly.

If your child is old enough to understand, you should instruct him or her that the animal's aggressive behavior was due partly to his or her own action. If you can teach the child not to provoke the pet, it is possible that the aggressive behavior by the animal will disappear. Steps for training a child to safely and gently interact with a dog or cat were discussed in Chapter Nine.

However, no matter what the reason for it, any aggressive action by your pet towards your child is a serious matter. Even if you are able to correct the causes of one particular incident, there is no guarantee that your dog or cat will not respond aggressively when confronted with a different set of circumstances. You should seek professional help immediately. Your pet's aggression may be correctible. Your veterinarian, an animal trainer or a behavioral specialist can lead you through your options that will ensure the safety of your child and allow peace to return to your home. Until such time, however, it would be best to keep your pet and your child separated.

Appendices

Appendix A
The Right Pet
For Your Family

If you do not already have a pet, you may be thinking about getting one. Before doing so, you need to consider several issues. The first one is timing. When a child is part of the equation, your decision on when to get a pet is crucial. Once you have decided that you definitely want a pet, you will need to pick the type of animal, the breed and the age. Dogs and cats are the most common domestic animals; however, there are many other animals that make suitable pets for your children. The information in this appendix will help you organize your thoughts so that you can make the best decision for your family.

When To Get a Pet

If a member of your family is pregnant, it is not a good time to get a pet. Any animal will need a period of time to become accustomed to its new environment. And then just as your pet has adjusted, a new baby will arrive and throw the household into confusion. Puppies are particularly difficult. A two or three month old canine requires an exorbitant amount of attention, just like a newborn baby. It is a rare individual who can cope cheerfully and successfully with a wailing baby and a crying puppy at the same time.

Another bad idea is to get a pet while a mother is on maternity leave. A new mother does not have enough time or energy to adequately care for a new pet. This is especially true with a puppy. Many people mistakenly believe that they will be able to housebreak and train a puppy during their time at home. Instead, they find themselves too busy with the baby. Besides this, a dog should be old enough to have completed its obedience work before the baby's arrival. If it has not been trained, the parents may not be able to properly control the animal when it is around their child.

Many people get a dog or a cat when their child reaches the toddler age; their theory is that having an animal around would be good for their child. The belief is correct but the timing is wrong. Toddlers are not able to restrain themselves sufficiently with an animal. The child or the pet may get hurt.

Getting a puppy or a kitten for a toddler is even less sensible; a young animal will share the toddler's lack of understanding and self-restraint. A child who is nipped by a boisterous puppy or scratched by a playful kitten may become fearful of animals. This would defeat the reason for getting the animal. It is better to bring an animal into the family when the child and pet are better suited in age.

The best time to get a pet such as a dog or cat depends on the maturity level of your child. He or she may be ready for a dog or cat around the age of five to seven. However, an adult will need to be the primary caregiver. Most children will have to be at least ten years or older before they are ready to assume any significant responsibility for care of a family pet.

If you want your very young child to have some experience with a pet, you may wish to acquire a "first" pet that is easy to care for and requires little attention. When your child is between the age of infancy to about four or five years old, a low-maintenance animal may be the best choice. Fish, guinea pigs, hamsters and gerbils make nice pets. You can put the cage or tank in your child's room and your child can learn by observing it. With some of these animals, your child may be able to touch or hold the animal while you supervise.

Selecting the Type of Pet

Several factors should be considered as you select the type of pet that is best for your family. The first consideration is time. All pets require some attention and care from their owners. However, the amount of time needed for these activities varies with each type of animal. You should pick a pet whose needs can be properly met in the time that you have to give it. For instance, some pets such as fish, hamsters, gerbils and mice need little attention except for feeding and an occasional cleaning of their cage or tank.

A dog requires much more time. It will need to be exercised and will require several trips outside each day. All dogs also need to follow set routines. The lack of this attention or a constant change of its daily regimen may lead an animal to misbehave or become destructive. In addition, you will need to make arrangements for a dog's care if you decide to go away without the animal. A dog cannot be left in the house for long periods of time.

Cats fall somewhere between a pet needing limited attention and one that requires a relatively large block of time each day. The amount of time needed is set by each cat individually. Some are content with little human contact; others are as social as dogs. In addition, a cat can do well if you need to leave it for a day or so. Dry food will stay fresh for that length of time; the litter box will allow the animal to relieve itself without going outside.

The second consideration is the amount of space that is available for a pet. Pets such as birds, fish, rodents or rabbits require little space. The extent of their home environment can be the confines of their tank or cage. Those that need exercise can be let out at periodic intervals.

On the other hand, a dog needs room. In all likelihood, the inside of your house will not be enough space, no matter how big it is. The amount of space required is determined by the size of the animal and its temperament. An indoor pet will not have enough room unless it is walked frequently. With proper exercise, however, most dogs adjust well to their living conditions.

A cat usually does not need as much space as a dog and can adapt well to indoor living. However, a feline will try to claim its environment as its territory and will want to roam within it. If you do not want an animal wandering around your home at will, a cat may be the wrong pet.

A third major consideration in selecting a pet is determining how much contact you want with the animal. If you want to keep a pet and child separated, you should consider a confined animal. While a fish is in its tank or a rodent is in its cage, it can be observed by your child but will not be subjected to unwarranted attention. In this fashion, both the child and the pet will be safe.

A dog is a social animal. It will want to constantly interact with the family. This interaction, while providing a feeling of security for both the animal and its family, can lead to trouble. A dog may remain in the presence of a child who is annoying it until the animal reacts in an aggressive manner. However, proper adult supervision between a dog and a child should enable you to avoid an incident such as this.

A feline is a different matter. A cat generally leads a solitary life. It will interact with your family only when it wants to and will usually walk away if your child bothers it. While some are very social, others shun almost all human advances. If the cat is very aloof, your child may not be able to have a close relationship with your pet.

Once you have evaluated your particular needs, you can choose the type of animal that is best suited for your family. A properly selected animal will provide years of happiness and will have beneficial effects for both the animal and your family.

Dogs

If you decide that you want a dog, the biggest issue that you now face is what kind to choose. You should use similar criteria to choose your dog as you used to select the type of pet. The amount of time that you will have each day to devote to your dog should be considered. Dogs that have been bred for outdoor activities will require more exercise than a small lap dog. And while all dogs need to be groomed on a regular basis, long-haired breeds may require more time than a busy household can muster.

As mentioned earlier, the amount of space needed by a dog is determined by its size and temperament. An animal living inside should be able to move about the home or wag its tail without continuously bumping into furniture or knocking things over. In addition, the space should fit the dog's activity level. For instance, a large, placid

Great Dane may thrive in a small apartment as long as it can comfortably move about and is exercised on a regular basis. However, a small, active Scottish Terrier may not do well in an apartment of the same size if the home is too small to allow the animal to expend its constant energy.

You should also consider what role you want the dog to play. If you want a dog simply to be a companion, you should concentrate on those breeds noted for gentle temperaments. However, you may be considering a dog that will provide protection for your family. If so, be very cautious. Any guard dog can be dangerous and may attack the wrong person, including your child.

Once you have identified the criteria for your selection, you can begin researching the various breeds. The best resources are books, your veterinarian and somebody who has the same type of dog that you are considering. Although some generalizations can be made about each breed, all dogs are individuals and should be evaluated on their own merits. For example, many pet owners have found that Golden Retrievers are gentle with children and that some terriers tend to be too active for youngsters. However, there are Golden Retrievers that are aggressive and terriers that are docile. A breed's reputation is helpful but it should not be the only benchmark.

Besides purebreds, there are countless variations of dogs. These are the mixed breeds or mutts.

A great deal about the lineage of a mutt can be learned from its physical characteristics. By identifying a bit of its genealogy, you may be able to guess the temperament of a mixed breed dog. Many mixed breed dogs are very intelligent and make wonderful pets.

Puppy or Adult

Once you have chosen the breed, you must then decide whether you want a puppy or an adult dog. A puppy is adorable but it is truly like a baby. A very young puppy may keep you up at night. You will need time, energy and patience to housebreak and train a puppy. Young puppies and young children do not always mix well. Neither have full control of their actions. Aggressive playing with a puppy may hurt the animal and lead to your child being bitten. Constant teasing by a child can result in a mean adult dog. If you want a puppy, perhaps you should wait until your child is mature enough to know how to act properly around such a pet.

The other option is to obtain an adult dog. Older dogs are more mature and generally calmer than puppies. The main issue with an adult dog is that you may have a difficult time breaking any bad habits of the animal. You can teach an old dog new tricks but it requires a great deal of patience and persistence. Eventually, your dog should be able to behave in a manner that satisfies you.

Where To Get a Dog

The last decision that you need to make is where to get the dog. You can get a puppy from a shelter, pet store, private owner or breeder. If you choose a private owner or a breeder, try to select your pet before the animal is weaned. This will give you a chance to meet the mother. A breeder should be able to tell you about the father as well. This information may give you a few clues to your puppy's personality and behavior. Bear in mind, however, that behavior is a complex phenomenon; it is shaped by the environment of a dog as well as its genetic background. Regardless of how much you learn about the lineage of a puppy, you cannot be sure that the animal will develop in the same fashion as its parents.

Adult dogs are obtained through a variety of sources. If you are considering adopting a dog from another family, you should ask the current owners several questions. These can help you determine if that particular animal meets your needs. Some are listed below.

- Why is the family giving up of the dog?
- How much obedience training has the dog had?

- Has the dog ever been exposed to children? How did it react to children of various ages?
- Has the dog ever had any behavioral problems? If so, what were they and how were they corrected?
- When was its last visit to the veterinarian? Are its inoculations up to date?

Adult dogs are also available through rescue programs. There are voluntary organizations that try to keep dogs out of shelters when their owners are unwilling or unable to care for the animal any longer. These generally deal with a specific breed.

Animal shelters are a third source of adult dogs. A dog adopted through a shelter is inexpensive compared to an animal purchased from a breeder. However, you may have limited information about the dog's background. Many canines available through a good shelter are healthy, neutered and have current inoculations. The best reason for getting a dog from a shelter is that you will probably be saving its life. Shelters can maintain their animals for a limited period of time. Animals that are not placed in homes are eventually euthanized.

After getting your new puppy or dog, you should make an appointment to visit your veterinarian. The doctor can give your new pet a complete physical and update the immunizations that the animal received from the breeder, rescue program or shelter. After the animal has been cleared by your veterinarian, your dog is ready to join your family.

Cats

If you have decided to get a cat, there are over 30 breeds from which to choose. The best resource for learning about a particular breed is someone who currently has a similar cat. That person should be able to answer most questions about the cat's personality and behavior. Of prime importance is finding out how the cat reacts to children. Other good resources are your veterinarian and the many books on the subject. Just like evaluating a dog, however, you cannot judge the quality of a cat or kitten as a perspective pet by its breed alone. Each cat is an individual. Wide behavioral differences exist between cats of the same breed.

Also like dogs, the most frequent sources of cats and kittens are breeders, other families, rescue programs and shelters. You should learn as much about a perspective pet as possible. This information may include meeting the mother of a kitten, finding out why a family is giving a cat away and how long the animal has been in a rescue program or shelter. Have the animal examined by your veterinarian immediately after taking possession. Your veterinarian can update your cat's vaccinations and insure that it is in good condition. This will minimize the chance of the animal being a health risk to your family.

One major health concern is the spread of toxoplasmosis. Toxoplasmosis is a parasite that poses a great risk to an unborn child. A pregnant woman exposed to toxoplasmosis may experience complications. Fortunately, toxoplasmosis can be avoided by families that already have a cat. As a general safeguard, however, a new cat should not be brought into a household if someone in the home is pregnant. It would be better to wait until after the baby is born. Toxoplasmosis is discussed in more detail in Appendix B: Zoonotic Diseases.

Other Animals as Pets

Some people decide that they want a more unusual pet than the typical dog, cat or caged animal. One pet gaining in popularity is the ferret. Ferrets, under proper supervision, can be good pets. However, they can be aggressive and bite if not handled correctly. Several cases have been documented where ferrets have bitten babies when the infant's extremities smelled of milk or formula. If you want a ferret for your family pet, it should be kept caged or closely supervised at all times. The animal should never be loose around an infant.

Other people have tried to adopt a wild animal, such as a raccoon or a fox, as a pet. That is a bad idea. Wild animals are not domesticated and should not be brought into a household. While they are cute and cuddly as babies, they often grow to display the same tendencies as their relatives in the wild. The biggest concern is rabies. Wild animals cannot be vaccinated for the virus. If a wild pet bites someone, either the animal must be destroyed to test for rabies or the bite victim must undergo a series of injections to prevent the disease. Last, in most areas, the keeping of a wild animal as a pet is illegal.

Appendix B
Zoonotic Diseases

Zoonotic diseases are illnesses that are shared by animals and people. The chances that your child will contract a disease from your pet or another animal are remote. Most illnesses are spread between species. In other words, a dog will usually only be infective to other dogs; people will usually only be infective to other people. But there are some illnesses that your pet or another animal may transmit to your child. These diseases are generally easy to treat and even easier to prevent.

Of the 30 or so zoonotic diseases, only about a third are addressed in this appendix. Those that were mentioned in Chapter Three, Good Health Care, are expanded to give more detail. Some of the other more common zoonotic diseases are also discussed.

Rabies

The most dangerous zoonotic disease is rabies. Rabies is caused by a virus which attacks the nervous system of mammals, resulting in inflammation of the spinal cord and brain. It is transmitted to a recipient through the saliva of an infected mammal. Rabies cannot be cured in pets or people once the virus has entered the central nervous system. Left untreated, it results in a painful death.

Depending upon how the virus is affecting the animal, the disease is classified as one of three stages. The first is the prodromal phase, where the animal shows no symptoms. An animal bitten by a rabies carrier may not exhibit any signs of the disease until several months after being infected.

The furious phase (also known as excitatory rabies) results in frantic behavior. This is when the classic image of the "mad" dog may occur. Animals in this stage are prone to launching unprovoked attacks and biting at both animate and inanimate objects.

If the animal has become unnaturally quiet and depressed, the disease is said to be in the dumb phase (also known as the paralytic phase). Its activities and energy level will drop significantly. As the disease progresses, animals may develop a dropped jaw, ataxia, progressive paralysis and convulsion. Animals die within several days of the onset of these symptoms.

The symptoms exhibited by a person with rabies vary, depending on where the virus entered the body. Bites to limbs can result in localized paralysis shortly after infection. Regardless of the location of the wound, however, the virus will eventually affect the central nervous system. Once the virus enters the spinal cord, the victim will suffer from paralysis that progresses as the disease spreads up towards the brain. The eventual outcome is death by respiratory paralysis.

It is possible for a person to be vaccinated against rabies. However, most pet owners are never exposed to the disease. The only people who routinely receive the vaccinations are those who work with animals. These include veterinarians, zoo keepers and animal control personnel.

Fortunately, the vaccine for pets is extremely effective and causes few side effects. Vaccinations are generally administered at 12-20 weeks of age for a puppy or kitten and repeated at intervals of one to three years. Your veterinarian will give you a certificate with a renewal date. As long as its vaccination remains current, your pet cannot contract the virus and subsequently cannot transmit the disease to a member of your family.

Besides vaccinating your pets routinely, you should also avoid handling any wild animals. The most common carriers are raccoons, foxes, bats and skunks. (Stray dogs and cats are also at risk but the number of cases is fairly low.) You should also teach your children never to approach any wild animal. Your pet's exposure to these creatures should be restricted as well. Even a friendly animal can be extremely dangerous.

If your pet is bitten by a wild animal or any animal that does not have a current rabies vaccination, contact your veterinarian immediately. If your pet has a current vaccination, it may need a booster shot to increase its protection.

If your child or you are bitten, the first step is to wash the wound with plain soap and water. Since the rabies virus is transferred through an infective animal's saliva, cleaning the bite area will drastically reduce the chance of contracting the disease. After cleansing the wound, you should contact your physician.

Next, all circumstances surrounding the bite must be examined to decide a proper course of action. Dogs and cats must be caught and quarantined for 10 days. If the animal does not exhibit any symptoms during the confinement, it is considered free of the disease and, therefore, no risk to a person. However, if the virus is in the saliva and the animal is infectious, it will show other symptoms of rabies during the 10 day period.

If the animal is suspected of having rabies, it must be tested; so must wildlife and stray animals. The most common and accurate test requires samples from the animal's brain. Thus, it must be killed. If the test is negative, you will not need to be treated for the disease. However, if the test is positive, you will be given a series of preventive injections.

If the animal that bit cannot be found, you must procede as if it was infective. In a case such as that, your physician will probably administer the preventive injections as a precaution.

Toxoplasmosis

Another frightening zoonotic disease is toxoplasmosis. It is caused by a parasitic organism known as Toxoplasma. The disease can be contracted through eating raw or undercooked meat that is infected with the organism. Toxoplasmosis is also carried by cats. It can be transmitted when a person inadvertently ingests the parasite after coming into contact with cat feces.

Studies have shown that almost one third of the women of childbearing age in the United States have been exposed to toxoplasmosis at some time in their lives. For most women who are exposed, there is no danger. They develop an asymptomatic infection that clears; their bodies create antibodies and become immune to reinfection.

However, if a woman contracts the disease when she is pregnant, there is a 20-50% chance that her fetus will be infected as well. It is estimated that over 3000 infected children are born each year in the United States. Birth defects resulting from toxoplasmosis can be devastating; they include mental retardation and blindness.

Ideally, a woman who has regular contact with cats should be tested for toxoplasmosis before she becomes pregnant. A positive test means that she has already been exposed and there will be no risk during the pregnancy. A woman that has become pregnant before testing should consult her health care professional for advice.

A pregnant woman should take steps to avoid the disease. One of the easiest ways is to avoid eating raw or undercooked meat, especially pork or mutton. She should also thoroughly wash her hands after handling raw meat or the utensils used to prepare it. Garden vegetables must also be washed to remove any traces of contaminated soil.

Even though the results are not 100% accurate, her cat should be tested for the parasite. If the cat is clear, the animal should be restricted from going outside for the duration of the pregnancy. If the cat is not allowed to hunt infected prey and not fed raw meat, it cannot contract or transmit the parasite.

It is not necessary to get rid of the cat if it is carrying the organism. It can be treated, although there is no guarantee that the treatment will totally eliminate the infection. Instead, a pregnant woman should take precautions herself. First, she should wash her hands after handling or petting her cat. Second, since the parasite does not become infective until 1-5 days after being excreted in the cat's feces, the litter box should be cleaned every day. It is best that the woman does not handle this job. However, if she must, she should wear gloves. She should also wear gloves whenever gardening or working in the yard. Many cats use flower beds and other areas as outdoor litter boxes. Even if wearing gloves while cleaning a litter box or working in the yard, a pregnant woman should wash her hands afterwards.

In addition, contact with other people's cats should be limited to those felines that are not fed raw meat and are kept as indoor pets.

External Parasites: Ticks, Fleas and Mites

Ticks, fleas and mites are parasites that can affect pets and people. Your dog or cat may carry these parasites into your family's environment and subsequently increase the chance that your children or you will be infested. The result of being bitten can be painful and itchy skin inflammation. Besides that unpleasant condition, a bite victim may also contract one of the diseases carried by external parasites.

Generally, ticks are not easily spread by dogs and cats because they attach themselves to their host. One that has bitten your pet probably will not fall off the animal and then bite you. While a pet may carry a tick or two into the house, it is more common for dogs and cats to serve as sentinel species. If you find ticks on your pet, there is a good chance that you have also been exposed to ticks and the illnesses that they carry.

One of the most talked about tick-borne illness today is Lyme disease. White-footed mice, birds and deer are the primary hosts of ticks that carry the illness. After feeding on of one of these hosts, an infective tick may then hop on another host who is conveniently nearby. This might be your pet or you. The first sign that a person may have contracted

Lyme disease is a red rash around the bite area. As the illness continues, the symptoms may include nausea, fever, aches, joint pain, inflammation and possibly meningitis. Extensive neurologic damage may also occur; in some cases, this has caused victims to lose the ability to walk. A pet that develops Lyme disease will not get a rash but will probaby have a fever. It may also become lame; the pain and inflammation will come and go from various joints. This can lead to arthritis. In both people and pets, Lyme disease is treated with antibiotics.

Another well-known illness spread by ticks is Rocky Mountain spotted fever. Despite its name, this illness is most prevalent in the southeastern states. Unlike Lyme disease, Rocky Mountain spotted fever is not transmitted only through tick bites. There is some evidence that a person can contract the disease by incorrectly handling an infective parasite. When it is removed from your pet, the tick may spit up an infectious substance. If you are not wearing gloves and the substance gets into an open sore, you may develop the illness. People and animals with Rocky Mountain spotted fever may have rashes, fever and loss of appetite. Other symptoms can include fatigue, disorientation and headache. Antibiotics are used as treatment.

If you find a tick on your pet, your child or you, you should remove it as soon as possible. Research has shown that several hours often elapse before many of the tick-borne diseases are transmitted from the parasite to the host. If you can remove the tick shortly after it embeds itself, you will reduce the chance of the bite victim becoming ill. For this reason, you should check your children and pets for the parasite every day during tick season.

In contrast to ticks, fleas are often transferred from a pet to its family. While the flea that bites your pet will probably not bite you, its offspring might. After the parasite has fed, it will begin to lay eggs. Within a few weeks, the eggs will hatch and the new fleas will develop into mature biting parasites. As the flea population grows rapidly, so does the chance of your family being bitten.

Infestation of people is short lived; fleas do not like humans as hosts. However, flea bites do create red, inflamed bumps and sores which are extremely itchy. Children often scratch the bites until they become infected.

Fleas can also transmit diseases. The most renowned is the plague. Contrary to popular belief, this disease did not die out in the Middle Ages. It is still prevalent, especially in the southwestern United States.

Wild rodents are usually the source of the plague. The illness is transmitted when an animal eats a contaminated rodent or is bitten by the rodent's fleas. A dog infected with the plague is usually not at risk; its illness is generally short-lived and does not require treatment. A cat may have a more serious infection; the animal often dies. There have been rare cases of humans contracting the disease from an infected cat. Being a bacterial infection, however, the plague can be effectively treated with antibiotics.

Another external parasite that can affect people is the mite. Like fleas, animal mites can be transmitted from a pet to a person. There are several kinds of mites that cause a variety of skin problems; these loosely fall under the heading of mange. The most common is sarcoptic mange. A person infested with mites will have irritated skin and many very itchy bumps. These most often develop where the edge of clothing meets the skin, such as the beltline and the cufflines of shirts and pants. Since people are the incorrect hosts for animal mites, the parasites cannot reproduce. As a result, a mite infestation is self-limiting. It usually clears up within a few weeks.

Worms

Most worms can only mature and reproduce in their specific hosts. So, you will only find adult dog worms in dogs and adult cat worms in cats. But there are some parasitic worms whose larvae (immature worms) can infect your pet and child. The most prevalent of these are roundworms.

Most dogs and cats will be infected with roundworms at some time in their lives. Almost all puppies and kittens are born with the parasite. (This is because nearly every adult animal carries the parasite in a dormant stage; pregnancy causes worms to become active.) Pets infected with roundworms can become very sick. Some of the symptoms may include weight loss, diarrhea, a distended belly, coughing, a rough hair coat and even depression. It is particularly common for infected puppies and kittens to display a potbelly.

You might be able to identify worms in your pet's feces or vomitus. However, the only way to know for certain whether your pet has roundworms is for your veterinarian to test a sample of your pet's fecal material, also known as a stool sample.

Roundworms cannot be transmitted to your child through direct contact with your pet. Hugging, kissing or being licked by an infected animal will not expose the youngster to the parasite. The only way that a human can contract roundworms from a pet is by ingestion of roundworm eggs. About four to five weeks after an animal becomes infected with round-worm, it begins to excrete the parasite's eggs in its feces. After 10 to 14 days in the dirt or grass, the eggs become infective. They can remain in this state for a period of several months. A child may inadvertently ingest the tiny eggs by swallowing or chewing the dirt that contains them.

If some eggs are swallowed, a child may contract a disease called visceral larva migrans. This is a condition where the roundworm larvae migrate to different parts of the body. Most children who get this infection do not even know it. The infection is self-limiting and requires no treatment. But some children do develop rashes, fever and coughs. In rare cases, the larvae migrate to the eyes; this is known as ocular larva migrans.

The best way to prevent roundworm infestation of your child is cleanliness. You can begin by picking up any animal feces as soon as possible. In this manner, the eggs do not have a chance to disperse into the grass and do not sit on the ground long enough to become infective. Next, instruct your children to keep their hands as well as dirt, sand and sandbox utensils out of their mouths. You should also teach them to wash their hands after playing outside.

Another important step is to have your pet checked and de-wormed often. Since almost all puppies and kittens are born with roundworms, very young animals should be wormed every few weeks. The feces of adult animals should be tested for roundworm eggs at least twice a year. If the test is positive, your veterinarian can prescribe medication that will rid the animal of the parasites. Repeated treatments may be necessary. You will need to be diligent in your de-worming efforts.

There are other worms that can be spread from dogs to humans. Hookworm eggs can also be passed in the animal's feces. The parasites are transmitted by direct contact with the human skin, usually the soles of the feet. A child with hookworms may develop skin rashes. You can help eliminate this risk by routinely cleaning your yard of your pet's stools. You should also have your child wear shoes whenever the youngster is playing in an area frequented by dogs and cats.

Many people are concerned that their children will get tapeworms. However, the varieties of tapeworms that infect pets do not usually infect people. Cat and dog tapeworms are often spread by fleas. Because a person would have to swallow a contaminated flea to get tapeworms, transmission from pets to people is very rare. The most common method of a person contracting a tapeworm infection is from the ingestion of contaminated meat.

If your pediatrician tells you that your child has intestinal worms, you should not automatically blame your pets. The most common type of intestinal worms afflicting people is the pinworm. It is contagious only between humans. Your pet can neither contract this parasite nor transmit it to your child.

Ringworm

Another illness that can be transmitted from an animal to your child is ringworm. Contrary to its name, ringworm is not a worm; it is a fungus that develops just below the surface of the skin. Its name is derived from its characteristic presentation as a raised, round, worm-like patch on the skin of an infected person.

The ringworm fungus grows on and in hair

follicles. For most animals, it causes hair loss and patches of naked, crusty skin. The patches tend to be about an inch or two in diameter. They are usually found on the face, head, or ears, but they can be anywhere (even on the toenails). If you suspect that your pet may have ringworm, your veterinarian can test a few hair samples for the fungus. Once diagnosed, ringworm can be treated with medicated shampoos, ointments and oral medication.

Ringworm is easily spread from animals to people, especially to those with less developed or incompetent immune systems. This group includes children. On a human being, the fungus usually does not result in patches of crusty skin. Instead, it tends to grow in a ring-like pattern. If your child has ringworm, your pediatrician can prescribe medication that will eradicate the fungus.

Cat Scratch Disease

One very unusual zoonotic disease is cat scratch disease. It has long puzzled researchers. The current theory is that it is caused by bacteria that are found under the claws and in the mouth of some cats. The bacteria have no effect on the cat but they can make a human very sick.

The disease is transmitted when a cat transfers the bacteria by scratching a person or by licking an open wound. In rare instances, it can be transmitted via bites. Children are common victims because they tend to play with cats and end up getting scratched. The period between the transmission of the bacteria and manifestation of the illness can be several weeks in length. The most prevalent symptoms are redness and swelling at the site of the scratch or bite, followed by red streaks up the limb. Other signs may include swollen lymph nodes, headaches, fever, fatigue and loss of appetite.

Most cases are self-limiting; the symptoms will dissipate without treatment. Once the illness is over, a person cannot get it again. However, severe cases may require hospitalization. The patient would then be put on antibiotics and possibly have the lymph nodes drained.

You can take steps to reduce the chance of contracting cat scratch disease. First, advise everyone to wash their hands after petting a cat. Next, handle all cats gently so as to avoid bites and scratches. If your child is bitten or scratched, you should clean the wound with plenty of soap and water. Do not allow your cat to lick any open areas of skin. In addition, you should consult your physician if anyone in your family is experiencing any unusual fever or swollen glands. And be sure to inform the doctor about any unpleasant encounters with the feline.

There is one last point about infected cats. They are only able to transmit the bacteria for two to three weeks. So, it is not necessary to get rid of the cat if a family member contracts cat scratch disease.

Strep Throat

Strep throat is the common name for a sore throat caused by a streptococcus bacteria. Strep throats are very contagious between people. Animals can suffer from strep throat as well but the infection is usually caused by a different strain of the bacteria. However, if a family has persistent and recurrent cases of strep throat, it is possible for the family to give the bacteria to their pet. If this happens, the pet may then act as a transient carrier and give the illness back to family members.

If you suspect this, you should contact your veterinarian. Taking a viable throat culture from your dog or cat to test for the bacteria is difficult. Most need to be put under general anesthesia for this procedure. Rather than testing the animal, your veterinarian will probably prescribe a treatment of antibiotics. If your pet is a carrier, the medication will take care of the problem.

Chlamydiosis

Chlamydia are bacteria that cause a disease known as chlamydiosis. Cats with this illness often develop conjunctivitis. If your pet has this condition, it will shed the chlamydia organism in its eye fluid. A person who comes in contact with the fluid and then touches his own face can contract the illness. This happens frequently to children handling infective cats.

You can help reduce the chance of infection by taking three steps. First, you should have your cat vaccinated to help prevent it from contracting the illness. Second, your children should be instructed to always wash their hands after playing or handling a feline. Last, any eye problem that your cat develops should be treated by your veterinarian immediately.

Leptospirosis

Another bacterial infection that animals can transmit to humans is leptospirosis. This disease affects many mammals, including pets, livestock and wildlife. It is spread in the urine, blood or tissues of infected animals and causes kidney failure.

Dogs should be vaccinated against leptospirosis. Dogs are at risk because they frequently come into contact with the urine of other animals. This often occurs when a dog smells the urine left behind by other dogs to mark their territory. Proper annual vaccination prevents infection with and the spread of this disease.

It is rare for a person to contract the disease. When it does happen, it is usually from swimming in contaminated water. Symptoms of malaise, headache, muscle aches and fever may occur about 10 days after exposure. Antibiotics are used to effectively combat the illness.

Index

About the Authors

Jane E. Leon, D.V.M., is a practicing veterinarian in the Washington, D.C. area. She also writes, produces and records the nationally syndicated radio feature, "Pets and People," for the Associated Press. In addition, she is the author of *A Dog for All Seasons* and *A Cat For All Seasons*.

Lisa D. Horowitz is an attorney with a Washington, D.C. law firm. She is currently working on two books that cover various aspects of family care. She is expecting her third child this fall.

INFORMATIVE AND FUN READING

__THE ANIMAL RIGHTS HANDBOOK by Laura Fraser, Joshua Horwitz, Stephen Tukel and Stephen Zawistowski
0-425-13762-7/$4.50
If you love animals and want the facts about how the fashion, food, and product-testing industries exploit animals for profit, this book offers step-by-step guidelines to save animals' lives in simple, everyday ways.

__THE RAINFOREST BOOK by Scott Lewis/Preface by Robert Redford   0-425-13769-4/$3.99
Look into the spectacular world of tropical rainforests--their amazing diversity, the threats to their survival, and the ways we can preserve them for future generations. This easy-to-read handbook is full of practical tips for turning your concern for rainforests into action.

__MOTHER NATURE'S GREATEST HITS by Bartleby Nash
0-425-13652-3/$4.50
Meet the animal kingdom's weirdest, wackiest, wildest creatures! Learn about dancing badgers, beer-drinking raccoons, 180-foot worms, Good Samaritan animals and more!

__FOR KIDS WHO LOVE ANIMALS by Linda Koebner with the ASPCA   0-425-13632-9/$4.50
Where and how do animals live? How did they evolve? Why are they endangered? Explore the wonders of the animal kingdom while you discover how to make the Earth a safer home for all animals.

__SAFE FOOD by Michael F. Jacobson, Ph.D., Lisa Y. Lefferts and Anne Witte Garland 0-425-13621-3/$4.99
This clear, helpful guide explains how you can avoid hidden hazards--and shows that eating safely doesn't have to mean hassles, high prices, and special trips to health food stores.